Houdini Dog From HELL

Houdini Dog From
HELL

KIM LARSON

DEDICATION

To my grandson Devin:
A dog is only as good as the person training it.
May you learn from my mistakes.

ACKNOWLEDGMENTS

I want to thank both of my sons for all of the frustrating hours they devoted to running, walking, wrestling, chasing, being chased, dragged, pulled, picking up after and retrieving … the dog.

Had it not been for Buster's enthusiastic diversions and the mutual retaliation between himself and my sons, many of these adventures would not have taken place nor given us the many years of laughter.

TABLE OF CONTENTS

INTRODUCTION

Meet Buster. Typical Labrador Retriever. Full of energy—constructive or otherwise (usually otherwise)—social butterfly, playmate, thief, tormentor of my sons, delinquent and ... my worst nightmare. Sounds like another Lab story doesn't it? It is.

It was one of those times when I blurted something out, more or less talking to myself, but within earshot of my two boys: "We should have a dog. He could watch the house when we're gone. You guys would have a distraction instead of fighting with each other. It would teach you some responsibility."

That last part had repercussions beyond my comprehension. Boy, would hindsight have been a blessing if I knew what was to come!

I was a single mom with two boys, only nineteen months apart. Shannon was the oldest at ten. His bigger, younger brother, Casey, KC for short, would be nine in the Spring.

I guess they were all for it as they both talked excitedly at the same time. I only caught bits and pieces of the conversation so I figured I better get some kind of a plan to find this new canine member for our family.

I don't remember how I found this particular breeder. I called them and got the directions to their place. We hopped in the car and headed for western suburbia in the hope of finding that perfect addition.

Indian Summer in Minnesota was the ideal time of year when the frost kills off the blood-sucking mosquitoes, which many of us refer to as our State Bird, and the warm weather returns for maybe one or two more days before the arctic air moves in.

It was my favorite time of year. The temps could reach near eighty, but without the nasty humidity. As an added bonus, many of the leaves had already fallen off the trees and their dry aroma filled the air. This time of year should be bottled for use during those polar days and frigid nights of January and February. Since that wasn't possible, I put it out of my mind and focused on driving as the boys chattered about what they should name the new family member.

I found the place without too much trouble. Their driveway was tucked in between large bushes and I pulled in. They had an ample, wooded lot, surrounded by immense Maple and Oak trees that shaded the yard. We walked to the back where we saw the pen of puppies. Both parent dogs were on the premises and they all looked healthy and well taken care of.

Each of my sons had their eye on a particular puppy. The owners said it was okay to pick them up and take them out of the pen. They snuggled and giggled while the puppies chewed on their chins and licked their faces. As I held my own little bundle of fur, I heard my youngest son say, "Ooops. Oh, sorry little puppy." Just as I turned around I saw my son leaning down to pick up a puppy from the ground.

Evidently, he had jumped from my son's grasp and toppled on his head. He was the silliest puppy and had the most personality of all his siblings. My son gave me a look with his own puppy eyes. I guess the decision was made. He seemed to be a good choice, but seriously, how can you tell at that point?

I found the owner of the adorable little fur balls, "Looks like he's the one," I said handing her some cash.

My sons took turns holding him and snuggling against his wiggling little body.

"I'm sure he'll be an awesome dog," she replied.

"Thanks. I sure hope so," I said as we headed back to the car.

The ride home was one of the more peaceful trips made in that car. There wasn't any fighting for the front seat this time. They both wanted the back and there were no arguments as the puppy climbed back and forth between the two of them.

While they all played, I couldn't help but feel apprehensive about the whole situation. Being in agreement was not in their nature and I wanted to add a dog to that mix? What was I thinking? I made one quick stop for some puppy chow before we reached home. We finally arrived without incident—or accident—in the back seat.

As I got out of the car, I said to the boys, "Here we are guys. Let the dog sniff around. He probably wants to pee. By the way, do you know what you want to call him yet?"

"I know," Shannon said. "How 'bout Toby?"

KC chimed in, "Nah, that's stupid. We should call him Jake."

"And that's not stupid?" Shannon replied.

"Better than Toby," KC said.

3

"All right, that's enough," I said. "He looks like a Buster. What do you think of that?"

"Yeah, okay. That's good, Mom," they both responded.

That was way easier than I anticipated. I figured they would be at it the rest of the night!

I watched them chase Buster while he inhaled the scents around our two enormous Maple trees and the rest of the yard.

"Buster, come here little guy," said KC.

"Here Buster. Come here," said Shannon.

"Let's get him in the house. He's probably hungry," I said.

Shannon picked him up and carried him in.

Labs love people and attention—however and whenever they can get it. In time, it was not unusual to get a call from someone in the neighborhood that went something like this:

"Hi, do you have a yellow lab named Buster?"

I always hesitated, worried about what was next?

"Yeeaaah, and who is this?" I asked, wondering what part of town they were calling from.

The answers were always different. It appeared that Buster could always find a new and improved way to entertain himself. For example: "He followed my daughter home from school." Or "He jumped the fence into our yard." And I loved this one, "This is the County library." (OH, NO!)

The replies went on and on. So let me start from the beginning ... PUPPY-HOOD.

CHAPTER 1

OBEDIENCE CLASS

Like most puppies, Buster was rambunctious. He did all the normal puppy stuff, like playing with your socks—while they were still on your feet. Do puppies try to remove them, toes and all? He was a barrel of laughs.

On one unusually cold, Saturday morning, I decided to try to get some kind of order in the basement. Since the boy's hockey season was over, I could get their equipment packed up and out of the way. I had already washed their jerseys while they were out playing. I used minimal detergent and no dryer sheets so they couldn't tell. Then I put them back in the bag to get some of the hockey bag odor back and disguise that fresh, laundered smell that may have lingered. I guess it's a guy thing to have the worst smelling hockey gear. My oldest took it so seriously that he said his jersey made him gag when he pulled it over his head. Eew! I took his word for it and held it at arm's length when I dropped it in the washer—and let it sit there for a good soak.

Even though the washer and dryer entailed the chore of doing laundry, they were great tools, in more ways than one. They created clean clothes to be put away by boys that did not want to put clean clothes away. Therefore, the laundry appliances were tools to convince them otherwise. Red articles bled really nice onto white articles, if ya' know what I mean. Not putting clean clothes away meant wearing pink socks and underwear to school. I know, it was mean, but a single mom needed help any way she could get it (heh, heh). Besides, it only had to happen once.

So now with the two hockey bags out of the way, I claimed some of my laundry/work area back, but before I could make use of it, the boys had set up their race track set next to the ironing board so I couldn't get near it. (Good. One less thing I had to do).

With four feet of oblong track, the two boys sprawled on the floor with Buster, who had already grown considerably and was almost a year old. He watched them intently. I lost my space as fast as I had found it. Oh well. It wasn't the first time I had to step over kids and dog and it wouldn't be the last.

They had their track set up and started the cars running. Buster jumped up and watched the cars as they whizzed by. I didn't notice at first, but he looked like he was actually studying them as they went around and around. Without any success, he tried to grab one of the cars as it went by. They went by too fast. He couldn't catch one. Initially, I didn't pay much attention, but then I noticed he had hopped inside the circle, like he knew he had to calculate another way to grab one of those cars. He evidently figured out that he had a better chance if he was inside the circle. Who would have thought he had that kind of reasoning?

Once inside the track, he could spin in circles which enabled him to have a better chance of catching one. As he got closer to grabbing one of them, his nose found out there was an electrical current running through the track. "YELP!" But that didn't stop him from trying.

What a good sport. My boys adored him. And so did I—at first.

Since space was restricted, I decided I could be more constructive if I went upstairs and looked for something to rustle up for lunch. With my head stuck in the fridge, I stared blankly at the containers. Hmm ... All of sudden I heard the boys screaming, "Buster! Get back here!"

I could hear them clamoring over each other as they fell up the stairs. I turned to see what happened just as Buster rounded the corner at the top of the stairs with a race car in his mouth. He finally caught one.

"Oh no you don't!" I said as I grabbed the scruff of his neck when he tried to run by. "Drop it!"

It took a few seconds to get it out of his mouth.

"Here ya' go guys! How did he manage to catch one?" I asked.

Shannon, the oldest, replied, "I don't know. All of sudden Buster jumped over me and ran up here. Then we noticed one car was gone."

He took the car back and headed back downstairs.

"Stupid dog!" KC said as he started down the steps. Evidently, he wasn't stupid at all. They just didn't appreciate that Buster wanted to play, too.

I kept Buster upstairs and out of trouble while I busied myself in the kitchen. He must have gotten bored because he found another one of his peculiar habits to annoy everyone. We used to think it was cute when he laid on his side on the kitchen floor and played with the door stop. Not anymore. It was the type that screwed into the wall with a rubber tip on one end and nothing but a spring in between.

Boing, boing, twang, boing, twang, twang boing! That door stop kept him amused for what seemed like hours. Even though we knew his whereabouts and we were happy that he wasn't pulling our socks off our feet, we were ready to take him back to his parents. He looked adorable, but it was the most annoying sound and made it extremely difficult to focus on anything else since you could hear it no matter where you were in the house. It got old real fast.

"Buster. Stop that!" I was perturbed. He didn't even look at me.

"BUSTER! Here. Have a little treat." I handed him a piece of tomato. He came over to the counter and took it. Rather than gulp it down, he dropped it and picked it up a few times like he didn't like the feel of it. (Jello was another fun one to watch. He barked at it and knocked it around with his nose first). He ate the tomato and claimed his spot in the middle of the floor like a speed bump. He only did that when I was in the kitchen cooking.

Things were going along pretty well once I temporarily unscrewed the door stop, but it came to my attention that he needed obedience training. I figured that out on my own when he did everything BUT give me his undivided attention when I tried to teach him something. We enrolled him in a Level 1 obedience class and that's when the fun started.

He was a year old now. A big boy. A hand full. Since it was just me and boys, I was the unfortunate one who the training was bestowed upon.

It started out innocent enough. A simple command like "sit," created only a short delay in class as I had some minor difficulty, like being totally ignored. I thought maybe a more assertive or aggressive tone might give me better results. Maybe with a little added glare.

"Buster, SIT!" I said with the most intimidating look I could muster.

Hmm .... Still ignored, but I think he watched out of the corner of his eye. I was suspicious now and filed that away for future reference.

At that point, everyone in class completed their "Sit" command and was waiting and watching us. Our small delay had escalated into a major display of "who's really in control." I was frustrated and irritated to say the least. All right. They did it and so will we! I will not be bested by Buster!

I thought maybe he needed a little brute force to convince him that I was in charge. I tried pulling him down by his collar and pushing him over. I was so determined to get him to sit that I didn't realize I was rolling on the floor trying to pin him down. I caught a glimpse of the instructor and noticed she seemed quite amused since she stood quietly with her hands behind her back while holding back a smirk. Oh my, we had an audience. Okay then. I gave up, stood up, brushed myself off and gave her a helpless look, as she then said, "Okay, would someone like to volunteer their dog? How about you?" she asked without any hesitation and looked straight at me. It sounded like a plan to me.

"Sure, he's all yours. You can keep him," I said.

"Bring him up here please," the teacher demanded.

I brought Buster to the front of the class. She was nice about it though. She waited 'till I got back to my spot so I wouldn't miss anything as Buster walked behind her, stopped at her right side and looked at me, apparently showing off. I couldn't believe it.

"Buster, sit," she said.

I almost lunged at him as his butt hit the floor!

"ERGH!" I said frustratedly and a little too loudly. "Wait 'till I get you home!"

The rest of the class went pretty much the same way. It was like steer wrangling without the horse and rope. I sure could have used a rope. My luck, I'd have it wrapped around me somehow with Buster standing over me looking innocent and victorious at the same time.

When our little wrestling match was over, I tried to think of something good that came out of it. Oh, sure. We were great entertainment for the class. On the way out, I grabbed a booklet from the sign-in table. *Leader of the Pack.* Maybe that will shed some light on the subject. Looks like we had some homework to do.

Chapter 2

Rubs and Grubs

Buster. Had I known he would grow into his name, I would have decided on something a little more placid like, Buddy, Mellow Yellow, or Toby (like Shannon first suggested). There's nothing I can do about it now.

I picked up the booklet and scanned the Table of Contents.

Well this sounds interesting, I said to myself.

I flipped through the pages 'till I got to the chapter on "How to Establish Yourself as Alpha." Hmm... intriguing. To establish myself as alpha, I had to get him on his back and grab his throat—with my teeth? Fat chance. I can't even get him to sit. I had to come up with some kind of a plan. How am I going to get him on his back? Oh, I got it!

"Oh Buusterrrr. Want a belly rub?" Heh, heh, heh!

I could hear him bounding toward the dining room where I formulated my sinister plan.

"Come here, bud. Would you like a nice, relaxing massage?"

I got down on my knees and patted a spot on the floor for him to lay down. He made his way towards me, He was buying into it. I was so tickled. This could work. The possibility of having control over an intelligent, four-legged Tasmanian Devil was exciting, to say the least.

"Good boy," I said as I rubbed his belly.

Okay, this is it. I'm taking over as Commander. I kept rubbing his belly and casually bent over him, grabbed a mouthful of his neck (skin and fur) and bit him—gently. I didn't want to hurt him. For good measure I growled in case he thought I was playing around.

Sitting up, I spit some fur out of my mouth and pulled the rest off my tongue. Ol' Buster picked his head up and looked at me, and probably wondered why I wasn't rubbing his belly anymore. Does he even know what transpired here? Doesn't he know he's been demoted as Master of the humanoids? We'll see.

I waited 'till he got up. He just stood there and looked at me as if to say, "You okay? You have a strange look in your eye."

We stared at each other for a few seconds. Sometimes he had a strange look in HIS eye. I often wondered what he was thinking. He had to have been someone else in another life and came back to torment me. Little did I know, it appeared to be that way as time went on.

"Okay, Buster, SIT."

He did, after I repeated it a couple of times. But at least that was an improvement from our previous lesson. The actual evidence will be seen in our class next week. I can hardly wait. Until then, I decided to take it easy and unwind from the weekly stress of work, kids, and Buster.

Most Sunday afternoons before another work week started, I liked to watch a movie and take a short nap on the couch. That was the plan for this particular

Sunday. Since I made a large dinner around noon, I didn't have to worry about making a big meal later in the day. I could be a couch potato—at least for an hour or two. The boys were at their friend's house so a little R and R looked promising.

Buster was laying on the floor next to the couch, pretending to be a good dog. I had a coffee table there, but he had room to squeeze between it and the couch. Sometimes, I left a partially empty E oil capsule sitting on the coffee table. I used it to squeeze a drop or two on a cut or scrape to help it heal quicker and then left it on a coaster or piece of junk mail for next time.

For some reason, Buster liked to eat them. Just like he loved to eat Kleenex. Not the box of Kleenex. Oh no, he took the used ones out of the waste basket. I put a couple new ones in there once. Even crumpled them up to see if he knew the difference. He sorted through them and only ate the used ones. Must be some kind of canine nutritional value in boogers and snot.

Anyway, it happened there was a half empty E oil capsule sitting on the coffee table when I laid down to watch TV. I'm sure Buster knew that so he proceeded to be the loving, loyal dog and laid by the couch. HAH!

Since I knew what he was up to, I played along. For once I was going to be smarter than *the dog*. At least I liked to think that even though it wasn't true most of the time.

I stared at the TV but actually focused on Buster with my peripheral vision. He had his head down like he was sleeping. If he had been sleeping, there would have been snoring. Every so often he picked his head up and looked at the TV. The capsule was just a tad to his right. At least one of his eyes definitely checked it out. Then he put his head back on his paws as if to be disinterested. He reminded me of a periscope on a submarine, peeking his head up and down casually so as not to attract suspicion. Oh, he was a wily one. After a few more of those moves, he planned his next move.

In the past, he just stood up, grabbed the capsule and ran. I gave up chasing him because he usually swallowed it before I caught him. It's not like it hurt him to eat it. It was just the principle of the matter. I'm sure that's why he did it, too. So that's what I watched for, but this time, I think he wanted a little vengeance to get back at me for tricking him into a belly rub. He was going to pull another fast one and make me the dummy.

Buster, picked his head up again to look at the TV. He ever so slowly leaned toward the E oil capsule, and without turning his head, nonchalantly picked it up. Then, and this is when I discovered he had a rational thought process, a premeditated plan, a deliberate course of action, whatever you want to call it, he put his head back down and laid there quietly. I was stunned. I took a quick peek at him to see if he ate it. The capsule was gone but he laid perfectly still with his head on his paws. I couldn't help but wonder when he would make a run for it. What happened next was just as surprising.

Since he didn't make a run for it, I thought I'd just let him have the capsule, but then he stood up. I was ready to jump off the couch and chase him down, but he merely ambled toward the kitchen like he wanted a drink or a different spot to lay down. I was dumbfounded. I checked the coffee table again. The capsule was, in fact, gone. I searched the floor next to the couch thinking he dropped it. Not there. BUGGER!

I sprang off the couch. He heard me and took off. By the time I caught him, he had already swallowed it and stood there with a dopey grin on his face, apparently enjoying himself. Once again, he won.

God, what am I going to do with this dumb dog, who is obviously smarter than I am?

He's so smart, in fact, that he actually woke me up in the middle of the night once for a snack. Thinking he had to go out, I walked to the front door and opened it. Half asleep, I waited, but he didn't walk by. I then closed the door and walked back to see where he went. There was my buddy, Buster, standing in the kitchen next to the cupboard.

"What are you doing in here?" I asked him. "I thought you had to go out?"

He then stood in front of one of the lower cupboards and looked at it. I opened it and he stuck his head inside and touched the Graham Cracker box with his nose. For crying out loud—he got me up to get him a cracker. He ate one and left me standing in the kitchen holding the box of crackers while he went back to bed. That's it? One cracker? Damn that dog. He taught me another new trick.

CHAPTER 3

AUTO-EXERCISE

I recalled seeing a chapter near the beginning of that *Leader of the Pack* booklet about exercise. Evidently, adequate exercise helps your dog release pent up energy that could become destructive or obnoxious. Imagine that.

I couldn't expect the boys to exercise him all the time. They had homework to do and needed a little time to release their own pent up energy after being in school all day. And they needed time with their friends, too. None of that would happen if they had to exercise Buster. It would take too long.

Since there weren't enough hours in a day for me to walk or jog this fur-ball of energy, I had this brilliant idea of running him alongside my car. He's a smart dog (even though I called him the dumb dog). I only had to drive about six blocks and could then let him out to run the last three to the park. It was somewhat of a back road, not much traffic. This could be a plausible solution, I thought.

So one day after work, I loaded Buster into the back seat of the car. He assumed the position— elbow on the arm rest, head out the window, tongue hanging out. Ready for take-off. I drove a few blocks 'till I was away from the busier roads and pulled over to get out and open the back door. (Subsequently, I became so proficient that I could squeeze my left arm to the back and open the door without getting out. Terrific!).

As soon as his feet touched the road, I hopped back in the car, hit the gas and we were off. I clocked him at 23 mph on any given day. Now that's movin'! With that kind of speed, I scanned ahead to adjust my speed so we could make the only left hand turn without oncoming vehicles. Sometimes I had to slow down to block an oncoming car for him, but that was okay. I just looked like some crazy, woman driver cruising the park and I only got beeped at once.

I kept Buster aligned with the driver's side back door rather than behind the vehicle where he could get asphyxiated by exhaust fumes. The dog had enough issues upstairs without adding more brain pollution. I could also see where he was, while at the same time, he could hear my commands. It was a good system that worked quite well.

I steered him with voice commands as I drove and with an added hand, at times, to point the way. Apparently, something sunk in on our road trips. He knew "wait, left, right, back" and "that way." That was enough to get him to the park. As soon as we pulled onto the perimeter road, Buster cut across a hill and met me in the back maintenance lot where I parked the car and yelled out, "Buster, go doo-doo!"

By the time I got out of the car, I walked behind his favorite pine tree and picked up my prize. How exciting, eh? At least I didn't have to hunt for it. He was very methodical and consistent, I'll give him that. And I was the responsible dog owner. (For some reason, that sounded a little ironic). As there were few people that knew about the back lot, the next 45 minutes or so were his without human distraction. I sat in my car at the bottom of the hill and listened to the radio while I watched him run back and forth at the top of the hill. Sometimes he scanned ahead as he ran. Sometimes his nose was to the ground. Either way, he zipped back and forth like he knew what he was doing. Maybe he did.

Half a dozen songs later, I watched as he galloped this way, then galloped back the other way. After 20 minutes or so, I walked up the hill to help him out. He stood with his front paws on the water fountain looking for water. From previous excursions, he knew there was water in there somewhere. When I stepped on the pedal, the water shot way out, so he could drink without leaving behind the shoe strings that were hanging from his mouth. I envisioned some little kid getting a drink and walking away with Buster slimers stuck on the front of his shirt. Eew!

Once watered, I wandered back down the hill to my car and continued listening to the radio as I watched the sun quietly set. It was a peaceful, serene area even though it was only minutes from downtown. I could see the skyline in between the trees from where I sat. The shadows grew longer across the perfectly groomed golf course in the foreground to the left. To the right, the sun still glowed luminously on Buster as he gallivanted back and forth atop the ridge. How relaxing and peaceful it was here. How could one dog make life so chaotic and stressful? I looked to the top of the hill at Buster. He could, and he was damn good at it too.

I half sang along to the radio as I absentmindedly watched Buster. I supposed there was enough critter action in between our visits that kept his nose plenty busy. As I watched him with his nose to the ground, he was non-stop motion every which way, almost at the same time. It made me wonder what things smelled like to a dog. I didn't go any further with that thought.

I observed that his gallop turned to a trot, the trot into a lope, the lope to a walk. Won't be long now. He went back and forth 'till he finally fizzled out like a wet fuse on a fire cracker. I didn't have to whistle. He lumbered down the hill on his own. I opened the rear car door so he could hop in. Hop in? I considered myself lucky if he managed to get just half his body in. Usually, he got his front paws in far enough and stretched across the seat on his belly so only his hind legs were left out. Then he waited for me to lift the back end in. *My buddy, Buster!* I wish he could be trained as easily as I was being trained. Now that was just plain pathetic.

As soon as we got home, he dragged himself in the house and drank a bowl of water. No sooner had he left a slippery water trail from the bowl to his selected spot, he plopped himself down in the middle of the floor to, once again, be the kitchen speed bump.

I looked down on his limp body as his side raised up and down with slow, rhythmic breaths. He looked so peaceful and angelic as he slipped into dreamland. That's about the only time this dog was peaceful and angelic. Don't get me wrong, he could sit very still and appear to be a sweet dog, but it usually was an indication that all hell was going to break loose at any moment. That was dependent, of course, on how long it took him to figure out what he was going to do.

Well, no matter. He was quiet and peaceful for the time being. I enjoyed it as long as it lasted. Sweet dreams, Buster.

CHAPTER 4

PULLBACK PAYBACK

The end of the week approached and we were back in Obedience Class, all present and accounted for. The same people who observed Buster and I with amusement the week before, were back in their places as we waited for the instructor to get started. I felt their eyes were on us again, as if they half expected something to happen before we even got started. That could very well be. Buster was antsy and tried to pull me across the room to a cute little Beagle named Mindy. She was adorable, but had her own agenda as she nosed about the space around her owner.

I was already getting frustrated, so I grabbed one of Buster's treats out of the baggie in my pocket and opted to distract him 'till we got started. He didn't seem very interested until I managed to hold it under his nose. AHA! I finally got his attention. Should I try the "Sit" command under the stares of half the class on the other side of the room? Sure, I'm brave. Or stupid.

"Buster, sit," I told him as I prayed under my breath. He actually did—with a little help from me pushing his butt down. Whew!

The instructor took her place in the middle of the room and began our second class. All right, the moment of truth. We started with the review of the "Sit" command. That went well since he had a little preview before class started, only this time I didn't have to push his butt down. I think he actually caught on.

We worked through "drop" and '"leave it." That was a little tougher, but I thought it went rather well. At least I didn't have to wrestle him to the floor. We must have been a disappointment to the rest of the class. I noticed they didn't glance our way quite so often. No show tonight people. But one never knew what Buster had in store for us. He was too smart for his own good and I really believed he knew what vengeance was. Scary.

The rest of the classes flew by and we thankfully made it through each one without a major incident. Not to say there weren't a few minor incidents. We just made it by the seat of our pants, but he passed. I wanted to start right away implementing all we had learned so we could have a well behaved, four-legged member of the family. Not so. That's when Buster began to implement *his* plans.

Not too long after our obedience classes, Buster decided to dish out a little pay back. He loved chasing the boys or grabbing one of their toys and having them chase him. What great fun that must have been —for Buster.

As the boys grew, so did Buster. He almost outweighed both of them together, not to mention his four legs were quicker than their two legs, so I'm sure he wanted to take advantage of that. It all started innocently enough. Grab and chase, chase and grab. If the boys were rough, he got rough. If they got their toy away from him, he took it back. All in good fun, of course. One day, Buster got even.

KC had been running around the house with one of Buster's toys. The toy had went back and forth between them a few times already as they took it from each other, until KC realized Buster wasn't behind him anymore. He stopped to see why he hadn't caught him, yet. Rather than turn around and expose the toy to Buster, he bent over and peered back between his legs. There was Buster, a few feet behind him. Buster gazed at him with his dopey grin and waited for the opportune moment. From the basement I heard them running in their stocking feet, laughing and giggling, but just as suddenly, it turned to scrambling and screaming.

"AAAAHHHH! MOM, HELP!" I ran up the stairs two at a time to see what happened.

Buster had KC in a precarious predicament. Before KC could stand up from peering through his legs, Buster ran between them, grabbed his overly long shirt, pulled it back through his legs and proceeded to drag him through the dining room— backwards, and just slow enough so he wouldn't fall on his face.

That's when I came in. All I could do was laugh as KC was dragged around the dining room table. Did I detect a sparkle in Buster's eye as he went by? I think so. He knew what he was doing.

As we continued to practice Buster's commands, I decided to add a few hand signals. I wasn't surprised that he caught on rather quickly.

Okay, I thought. Let's have some fun and do something a little more creative. How about this? He should have an ID. Before we let him in the house, he had to show us his ID, his left paw. Hopefully, he'd forget so we wouldn't have to let him in. (If it could be that easy).

And how about this one? Sometimes he had to pay a toll for all the frustration he put us through.

That was his "other left paw." He was smart all right, and he caught on right away; but little did I know I had created a monster by challenging his mind that way. This is what our crafty, canine scholar did with his seemingly uninterested education. During one of his "social outings" I answered the phone and this is how the conversation went:

"Do you have a dog named Buster?"

"Ah, yes and I bet you're going to tell me where he is."

At that point, the voice on the other end said, "This is the County Library. Your dog is running around inside the library. Some of the kids knew him and let him in."

"Oh, no! Sorry about that. I'm only three blocks away so I'll be right there. Ah, don't let him check anything out. He doesn't have a library card!"

That crazy dog. Maybe he figured he could check something out with his ID. The boys had just walked in the house and one of them asked as I hung up the phone, "Who was that?"

"Don't take your jackets off. That dumb dog is running around in the library. Sounded like they were all having a great time so I may need some help rounding him up."

"How did he get in there?" asked Shannon.

"Apparently he has friends. They just opened the door and let him in!"

Five minutes later we pulled up in the library parking lot and saw Buster through the large window rounding a bookshelf with three giggling kids in pursuit. Then they all disappeared down another aisle.

"Okay guys, let's go capture the dumb dog," I said as I got out of the car. The boys followed with a hesitant look on their faces.

"Do we have to go in? We can wait here. We might see someone we know."

"Okay," I replied. "Stay by the door in case he somehow escapes."

As I walked in, I only had to follow the giggles to find the section he was in. How embarrassing. I headed him off at the next aisle and grabbed his collar.

"Hold on there, buddy. You're coming with me."

I walked Buster out as fast as I could, taking the path of least resistance so as not to not run into anyone, especially the librarian, who must have questions for me.

KC opened the door to let us out and Shannon opened the car door to deposit Buster in the back seat.

"Let's get out of here," I said as we headed for home.

CHAPTER 5

INDEPENDENCE DAY

It was the end of June. Summer was starting off absolutely perfect. Even though it was quite hot during the day, the humidity was lower than what it usually was this time of year and it cooled off comfortably at night. Who could complain? It was ideal. A summer to remember. Of course, up North, you usually remembered all of them. It's only a few, short months of sun and fun before the snow and frigid temps come back.

It seemed like no sooner had Memorial Day came and went that the Fourth of July was right behind it. It always came up so quickly. The Fourth was on a Saturday this year and the forecast called for a clear night. I thought about where we could go that would allow us to see the fireworks in different areas of the city from the same vantage point. I remembered the scenic overlook across from a cemetery near my previous job. It had a small parking area and lots of grass. We should be able to see fireworks in a few different directions at the same time. I decided that would be the best spot and suggested it to the boys.

"Hey guys. I have a great place to watch fireworks tonight. Remember where I used to work over by the cemetery?"

They had just came in the house and sat down at the table. In unison they answered without enthusiasm, "Yeah."

"If we sit up there on the hill, we should be able to see them all over the city at the same time!" I tried to get them to be a little more excited about it.

"That sounds cool," KC said.

"Yeah, okay," replied Shannon.

"How about going out for a pizza on the way over?" I asked.

Both of them perked right up. Now I had their attention. Just like dogs, food motivated them.

"Can we go to the place that has the good root beer?" Shannon asked.

"Sure. I love their root beer, too," I said. "Let's go, then!"

We hopped in the car and drove the four blocks to save time. Luckily, it wasn't busy yet so we were able to get our pizza and have two root beers a piece. They were small bottles.

After we finished our pizza we headed to the overlook about an hour before dark. Oh, and did I mention we stopped back at home first to pick up a blanket and Buster? That was my brilliant idea to see how he reacted to loud noises and a crowd of people.

We found a place to park and walked up the hill. We milled around 'till we found the proper spot and spread the blanket for the three of us and Buster.

I don't know why I put myself in these situations. I knew we were in a park-type setting: lots of trees, which meant lots of squirrels. Grass, with lots of scents. People, with lots of munchies. Good God, what was I thinking? I did put a little thought into it. I brought two leashes to hook together so he wouldn't be on top of us the whole time. I didn't suspect many squirrels to be running around with people walking about, but Buster still went after the ones in the trees, too. The one in our backyard taught him how to do that.

Once we were settled on the blanket, I turned to the boys and said, "Okay guys. Keep your eyes peeled for squirrels. We need to see them before Buster does."

"Yeah, okay, Mom."

They had a couple toys along with them so I knew I was on my own with that one. With the two leashes hooked together, I continued to scan the area for anything that moved while Buster casually got a nose full around the edge of the blanket. He sporadically tugged at his leash whenever someone passed by with their dog as he tried to greet them.

I eventually got him to lay down next to me. He had to be as close to the grass as he could get, though. He didn't want anything to get by him. He was finally settled enough that I thought I could get more comfortable while I kept an eye out for critters. I hooked the leash to my foot and relaxed. I watched the people as they walked by and selected their perfect spot to sit and enjoy the show. There was just a hint of a breeze and the air was still warm. I watched as the sun started to descend below the horizon and mused about the reddish-orange glow. Why is it a sunset can look so spectacular one evening and totally normal the next? Okay, define normal.

Oh, oh. I evidently let my mind wander. The next thing I knew I was being pulled off the blanket. SHOOT! I grabbed for the leash to get my foot out of the loop.

With the pressure of being pulled, I couldn't get my foot out. All I could do was holler for the boys,

"Guys, grab my arm!" as I reached back so they could grab me.

Luckily they were close enough. One grabbed my arm while the other ran after Buster to stop him.

That could have ended a lot worse, had it not been for the quick response and experience the boys had in Buster mishaps. He only dragged me about ten feet. It entertained enough people that a few of them got a good chuckle as the boys recovered our Houdini. Fortunately, sunset came before Buster tried anything else.

We watched the fireworks exhibition near and far. It was a spectacular show. We could see six or seven different areas around the city from where we sat. Even Buster behaved himself. I think he enjoyed the commotion in the sky. No wonder. He was a master at creating his own commotion. No more independence for Buster. At least not tonight.

As the different fireworks shows gradually ended, we made our way to the car and loaded Buster in the back. That meant one of the boys had to sit with him. That was always grounds for an argument.

Typically as soon as we walked out the door, whether it was at home or somewhere else, they started in.

"I call shot gun," one of them would say. If the same one called it first too many times in a row, then I had to pull rank to let the other sit in front to keep it fair. Either way, it was almost like a punishment to have to sit in back with Buster. Not that they had to worry about his slimers getting on them. They usually blew off or stuck to the side of the car. It was more like being in a side show when someone in the car adjacent to us noticed Buster with the wind blowing on his face. His eyes were pinned back and fluttering. His muzzle was flapping. The slimers stretched out of his mouth as long as shoestrings and he smiled to complete the ridiculous display. I guess I couldn't blame either one of them for not wanting to sit in the back with Buster. If we kept him behind me and I stayed in the left lane, they were spared his humiliating act of sheer, doggy delight.

We made it home without Buster attracting any unwanted attention. He was the first one to the back door so I knew he needed a drink. I unlocked the door and turned to the boys who trailed behind me.

"You guys can stay outside for a while if you want, but don't leave the yard. I'll call ya' in a bit."

"Okay," they chimed together. They were both happy to stay out.

I gave Buster his drink and watched him flop in the middle of the floor. Speed bump Buster. A perfect end to a perfect day.

CHAPTER 6

UNI-SLIDING

Time progressed quickly as I was busy with the occurrences of everyday life and the boys' with their school and activities. The weeks turned into months. Holidays came and went. Before long the days and nights got colder and colder 'till the snow fell.

Our two-story house sat reasonably high on a hill so our front yard looked down on the street. It was like our castle sitting up there. It provided an especially nice view around the holidays when the neighbors hung their lights and put their decorations out. We could look up and down the block and see almost every house across the street.

The hill was rather steep and a lot of fun to slide down. The only problem was that it was a real task to mow the lawn. It made me very appreciative of winter. Thankfully, the driveway in back was on the same level as the alley so it wasn't as much of a challenge as it could have been. It was bad enough having to shovel it and figure out where to put all the snow.

Winter was also a benefit when it came time to pick up dog-doo. I delegated that job to the boys. It wasn't that I didn't want to do it, but it allowed me to get other chores done that they weren't able to do. I know they didn't think it was fair, but I offered to pick it up if they vacuumed and scrubbed the floor. Or cooked dinner or did laundry. They begrudgingly agreed to take care of doo-doo detail.

Since it's such a thankless, degrading job, I decided to make it more interesting for them so they were more apt to get it done on a consistent basis. There it was. Another brilliant idea.

"Okay guys. I'm going to show you a quick and easy method to pick up dog doo. In fact, you won't have to pick it up at all."

They looked at me as if they doubted me. Imagine that. I grabbed an empty forty pound bag of dog food and headed for the door.

"Grab your jackets and come on outside. I'll show you my brilliant idea."

Okay, this time Shannon rolled his eyes and KC stared at me with that blank stare waiting to see what he had to do so he could get it over with.

"Watch and learn," I said. "This is all you have to do."

I took the empty bag of dog food, laid it on the ground and adjusted it to stay propped open.

"See? Simple," I said. "Now all you have to do is find a doo-doo pile and kick it in the bag. He shoots, he scores! Just make sure you clean your boot off when you're done."

I thought they would have been a little more enthused. They looked at me like I was bat crap crazy.

"Oh, come on. You don't think that was brilliant?" I asked.

KC answered, "Yeah, okay, Mom," and headed back up the steps to the house.

"That was your brilliant idea?" Shannon asked.

I was shocked.

"Yeah. It beats picking it up doesn't it?"

"Whatever," he said and walked back up the steps.

I trudged along behind them carrying the bag. I thought it was a great idea.

Winter in Minnesota had its challenges. Cold and snow. Add to that a thirty mile an hour wind and it feels even colder, not to mention you can get frostbite in one heck of a hurry.

But the good thing was that you had an extra freezer outside if the one in the house happened to run out of room. It worked really well to hide things in the garage, too, 'till the boys found out where the key to the freezer was. No cookie was safe in the freezer ever again. Too many times I went out to grab an ice cream pail of cookies, only to find the buckets were all half empty. They were quite ingenious. Rather than empty one complete bucket, they figured out that if they ate a little bit out of each bucket, I wouldn't notice it right away.

Speaking of cookies … I was up to my elbows in cookie dough one day when Buster needed to go out. The boys were close by, so I had Shannon put him out in the front. I chose him because KC was sometimes too easily distracted.

"Make sure you keep an eye on him and let him in right away as soon as he's done. It's pretty brutal out there with that wind," I instructed. Even though we had less than a foot of snow, it was extremely cold with the wind.

"Okay, Mom," he responded.

I peeked through the pass through window in the kitchen and noticed Shannon was on the porch watching Buster. It had only been a few minutes, so

35

Buster should be okay. I dove into the cookie dough and started filling up a sheet for the oven. Suddenly, I noticed no one was coming in. I washed and dried my hands and headed to the front porch to look out the window.

All I could see was my son out there wrestling with Buster. Apparently, Buster had slipped down the hill and couldn't get his footing. He was suspended by his neck on the hill and my son was trying to support him so he wouldn't hang himself.

I ran out the door and grabbed Buster to hold him up while my son unhooked the rope. Whew! That was a close one. Oh no. I turned to my son and asked, "How long was he suspended like that on the hill?"

My son answered, "Not very long. I ran out right away. Why?"

"I'm hoping there wasn't any oxygen deprivation."

"Oh," he replied. I could tell he wasn't sure what I meant but he didn't say anything as we ran back in the house. A few days after that, we had a major snowfall. More fun and games. It was always fun to play in the snow. Especially when you have enough of it to go sliding and live close to a big hill.

Sunday was a good day to get the crock pot full of chili and let it simmer while you were out playing. I decided we should all go sliding, but I did not understand the boys' apprehension and sullen faces.

"No, we don't want to go," said KC.

It sounded like whining. What was that all about?

"Come on, you need some fresh air and the dog needs some exercise."

"Yeah, that's what we're afraid of," Shannon said, "He'll get some exercise."

I ignored their opposition and managed to get everyone in the car. We got to the hill early afternoon.

There were quite a few kids there. Some looked like snow creatures after getting dumped off their ride on the home made jump near the bottom. I thought I heard one of them say, "Great, here comes that stupid Buster."

As we grabbed our plastic sled and walked to the top of the hill, Buster had already nabbed some poor kid's hat from his head just as he left for the bottom of the hill. The kids started to run after him, shouting "You stupid dog! Come back here!"

"NOOOO!" I yelled after them. "Don't chase him! You'll never see that hat again!"

Sheez, we hadn't been there two minutes and Buster was already in trouble.

"See, Mom?" KC said. "Now you know why we don't want to come here. Nobody likes Buster."

I had to admit, the other kids didn't look too happy. They had known Buster by name and avoided him like the plague. In another ten minutes, we might have the hill to ourselves, along with various outer wear.

I spent the next few minutes trying to get the hat back, which I finally did, only because he dropped it part way down the hill for a more enticing piece of winter wear. Mittens.

Buster took it as a personal challenge to gallop alongside a sliding apparatus and grab a mitten on the way down. Thank goodness for his gentle mouth. I quickly scanned the kids for any dangling scarves —just in case.

Buster was having a blast. He knew his boys and that he'd have a hard time getting anything off them, but he had to try since he was running out of unsuspecting kids. Unless some new faces arrived, his Run and Nab game was finished.

Not long after everyone left, we decided to go home, too. Buster had run up and down the hill so many times, it should ensure a peaceful evening.

We pulled into the garage and shuffled to the house. As soon as we were inside, our noses started to run, but we could still smell the chili that simmered in the crock pot. These are the good memories of winter.

"Hey, you guys want me to make some cornbread? Hot out of the oven with butter and honey," I asked.

"Yeah!" they both yelled at once.

After having our chili and cornbread, we decided to see what was on TV.

I wanted to find out if this nab and grab thing of Buster's was a routine event at the sliding hill.

"So," I said as I turned to the boys on the couch next to me. "How long has Buster been doing this kind of thing with the hats and mittens?"

Shannon answered, "It only happened a couple of times. We quit going there."

"Oh," I said.

"Yeah, but we took Buster there on the toboggan once. That was really fun."

KC added, "We sprayed WD 40 on the bottom. That worked good!"

Oh oh, I thought. I'm about to hear another hair raising adventure.

"Okay, do I really want to hear about this?" I said.

Ignoring me, KC said, "Remember when I had a sore rib? We hit the jump with me, Shannon and Dustin on the toboggan. We flipped it and I landed on the can of WD 40 in my pocket."

Shannon was chuckling as he said, "We went down the hill once with Buster, too. I think he liked it!"

KC chimed in, "Yeah, we put him in the front and I held on to him. When we got to the bottom of the hill, he jumped off, grabbed my hat, and ran back up the hill."

"That sounds like Buster," I replied.

I looked at him sacked out in front of the TV. At the mention of his name, he picked his head up and looked at me.

"Yeah, we're talking about you. Go back to sleep."

He dropped his head and did just that.

CHAPTER 7

MERRY SQUIRREL-MAS

In my mind, which I always believed was quite logical, I thought it better to grow IN to a house rather than OUT of it. Our four-bedroom house had plenty of room with nine foot ceilings to top it off. Since we had the room, I thought a large, real tree would be nice for Christmas. Something in the range of six or seven feet.

"Get in the car guys. We're going to get a real tree for Christmas!" I hollered and headed for the door. I grabbed my keys off the counter and noticed Shannon was right behind me. "Where's your brother?" I observed we were minus one.

"I don't know," he replied.

"He's probably outside," I said and shut the door after us. "KC," I called and locked the door.

We stopped when we heard a voice mumbling.

"Was that KC?"

Shannon shrugged.

"Hey Case! We're going to get a tree. You coming?"

We heard the mumbling again.

"What did he say?" I asked Shannon.

"I don't know," he replied.

"KC. Come on. We're going to get a Christmas tree," I called. Once again we heard a voice mumbling

41

something that sounded like the adults in a Charlie Brown cartoon.

"What is he saying? Did you get any of that?" I asked Shannon again.

He shrugged his shoulders. "No idea."

"Sounds like he's on the side of the house," I said and walked around the corner of the house.

Well that was a strange sight. Casey stood next to the house but wasn't moving.

"What are you doing?" I asked him.

He didn't turn around but started to mumble again. It all made sense now. Today was the day he decided to do what all kids do before they turn twelve: Stick your tongue on something metal in winter!

Being a single parent and not wanting my sons to grow up to be mommy's boys, I grabbed the hood of his jacket and yanked him off.

"AAAAHHHHH!" he yelled.

"Sorry but it only hurts for a minute and the tongue heals quick," I told him. "I did it, too. Left a little piece of my tongue on a metal rail at my grade school. You okay?"

"Na," Casey said but I think it meant 'No' because his tongue hung out of his mouth.

"We're going to get a real Christmas tree. That should take your mind off your tongue," I said.

We piled in the car and headed for a Christmas tree lot not far from the house. It didn't look too busy, so we parked the car and got out to find the perfect tree. After giving my specifications to one of the workers there, we were steered to some of the larger trees.

"Look guys. Check this one out. I think this is the one." It was the most perfect, pine tree. (Never could remember the difference between pine, fir, spruce or balsam tree). It had long needles, was full and … it had to be at least seven feet tall. It was a beauty. I turned to the boys, "Do you like it?"

"Yeah. It's really big!"

We had the guy load it on the car, and tie it down and we were on our way.

As soon as we pulled into the driveway, a thought occurred to me: *how on earth are we going to get this tree into the house?* If it was seven feet tall, it had to be at least six or seven feet around the base. I'm pretty sure the doors aren't that wide.

"Okay guys, we might have a little problem," I said as I parked the car. "How are we going to get this thing in the house?" I thought I heard crickets. I turned around and the boys had already bailed out of the car and were headed for the house.

"Hey, come back here," I said as I got out of the car. "I can't get this thing in the house by myself."

I saw them turn and shuffle back my way so I started to untie the tree. *Boy, this thing is going to be a real chore to get in the house* I thought. I had to think of some kind of plan. The back door looked pretty narrow and we would have to drag it through the house to get it in the dining room. The front door was a little wider, but then we had to drag it from the back of the house to the front. I suppose it was better for the tree if we didn't have to pull it through the smaller door. Like a few inches made a difference.

"All right. Here's what we're going to do. We'll drag it to the front and bring it in that way. We have to leave it on the porch for a few days anyway so it can gradually adjust to the temperature."

They gave me the deer-in-the-headlight look. I slid the tree off the car.

"I'll try to drag it by the trunk, but I'll need you guys to help me get it up the steps and on the porch, okay?"

"Yeah, okay," they said.

They didn't sound too enthused. I grabbed the trunk and started to pull. Shoot! Who would think this thing would be that heavy? I hadn't gone twenty feet and I was out of breath already. After numerous breaks to catch my breath, I made it to the front door. Then it got tricky. At the top of four steps was the door. I stood at the bottom and tried not to think how hard it was going to be to get it up those four little steps.

"Okay guys, get the door propped open while I get this tree lined up. I'm going to pull while you guys find a place near the middle to push. Try to push on the trunk and not the limbs so they don't break," I instructed.

"Okay." I thought, *this would be great if it worked.* What do I mean IF it worked? Of course it's going to work. Think positive, right?

"Here we go ... push!"

As I grunted and pulled, the boys did the best they could to push without getting stabbed by the pine needles or breaking the branches. That's when I realized my logical mind had been on vacation. Why do I do this to myself? This tree ain't goin' through this door!

"Mom, I don't think it's going to fit."

"Okay," I said. "Take a break and let's rethink this thing. Got any other ideas?"

They looked at me like I had horns growing out of my head. I gave them one of my own looks and said, "I think we got it to go a little way. Let's keep going. Once we get the base through, it'll go quick."

Now that was wishful thinking. I hope they believed it, because I sure as heck didn't.

With a few more combined efforts, we succeeded to pull the tree through the door and lean it up against the wall. We had a nice, three season porch. Cold enough for the tree to acclimate before bringing it into the house.

"Whew!" I was huffing and puffing. "As long as we're out here, get Buster so he can check this tree out so it's not a big surprise when we bring it in. You know how goofy he is with stuff."

Shannon opened the door. "Buster, come." Buster came running through the door. Immediately he went to the tree and inhaled it as far up as he could reach. Within a few minutes, he seemed satisfied and we all went in the house.

After a couple of days we were ready to bring it inside. We had one more door to go through to get the tree in the house. At least it was a considerably larger door and didn't cause too much of a problem squeezing it through. I brought all the boxes up from the basement so we could start decorating the tree. Once I got the lights on, I left the rest to the boys.

"Here ya' go." I set the boxes of ornaments down by the tree. "It's all up to you guys."

After I pulled out their Great Grandma's antique ornaments and hung them deep inside the tree for safety, I supervised from a distance to keep Buster out of the way 'till they finished. They worked diligently arranging the ornaments to cover up the spaces. They only had one casualty.

"Oh, oh," KC said. "Get the broom."

I swept up those pesky little, glass shards and stood back and gazed at the tree.

"Looks good! I like it. Plug the lights in," I said.

It was beautiful. With the star on the top, it was only about a foot from the ceiling. Buster liked it too, although he seemed more interested in the water underneath. *I hope that's not going to be a problem,* I thought to myself.

I positioned the tree in the dining room in front of the pass-through window to the kitchen. That way, we were able to see it from the living room and the kitchen. It was a perfect view, but not so perfect to keep an eye on the dog.

I had a few minutes to spare while I was cooking dinner one night and I leaned on the counter of the pass-through window to admire the tree. Through the tree I could see Buster sniffing around underneath. He was probably near the water again. What happened next still amazes me. I don't know what ever possessed me to do this, but I reached into the tree, grabbed the trunk, and gave it a little shake.

"Buster, get the squirrel!" I commanded.

Before I knew what had happened, he shot up the middle of the tree as I watched the ornaments fly off in all directions. That was the first mistake. The second mistake was the boys were right there and had witnessed the whole thing. Oh no.

"Grab that dog and get him out of there!" I shouted.

Though I never did that again, the boys thought it was hilarious to shake the tree and say "get the squirrel" while Buster was outside. Apparently, they loved to see the look of terror on my face.

CHAPTER 8

SNOW FIEND

Thank God Christmas was over and the week was half gone. With another chaotic drive home from work like that, taking the bus sounded like a good idea. Too bad I couldn't get there from home. As usual, everybody was in a hurry. I don't know how many times I heard someone beeping their horn. Fortunately, not at me. At least I didn't think I did anything stupid to warrant horn blowing.

I parked the car in the garage and ambled up to the house. I started work early enough in the morning so it was still light out when I got home. I unlocked the door and went in the house.

"Anyone home?" I asked.

"Yeah," Shannon answered from upstairs.

"Any idea where your brother and Buster are?"

"Who knows. They're outside, probably doing something stupid," he replied.

"I hope not," I said, but I kind of new better.

I started right in making dinner. Occasionally, I heard the upstairs floor squeak as Shannon moved about. He was probably digging something out of his closet.

It was a cold, winter afternoon and Buster and KC were outside doing something in it. It always worried me and my mind drifted through different scenarios of the kind of trouble they could find. One son and a delinquent dog with minimal adult supervision?

I tried to ease my mind and rationalized it by thinking it should only be two thirds the trouble since it was only two of the three. I knew better. That was the deciding factor for choosing to work early hours. They only had about twenty minutes from the time they got home from school until I got home from work. Not like that kept them out of trouble. I just found out sooner.

But it wasn't always the boys who instigated the trouble. Buster was an expert with his antics and they weren't always well received. Yet, on occasion, they were harmless and almost went unnoticed. I just wished he would stop bringing his stolen treasures home. I really didn't want some stranger banging on my door asking about things I couldn't explain. I mean really, who could explain anything Buster did?

I always knew when he had stolen property. He laid in the front yard with it. If he was halfheartedly chewing on something, it meant it was a toy or some piece of junk he picked up somewhere. Focused chewing meant it was food.

With our severe, cold temps in winter, I wasn't the only one who took advantage of it. Just step outside and you had frozen food at your doorstep. Apparently, some people didn't keep all of their food in a cooler because I remembered I caught Buster laying in the front yard chewing through a package of frozen hamburger. I guess we had to upgrade to a better neighborhood if he wanted steak. I felt bad to think he may have stolen someone's dinner. Bad dog!

I collected my thoughts and focused on the task at hand. I had dinner almost ready and was about to open the door to whistle for the two knuckleheads, when the door flew open. Buster came in and flopped on the first open space on the floor, which happened to be in the middle of the kitchen. KC was right behind him. He closed the door and fell back against it. His face was wet and beet red.

"What happened to you?" I asked.

He was so out of breath, he could hardly answer.

"Buster took … me on a ride ... from hell!"

Oh boy, here we go. What kind of trouble did that mean?

"How did he do that?" I asked.

"I hooked him up to our plastic sled," KC began.

I said, "Oh please don't tell me you were in the street?"

He gave me an incredulous look like, where else would you be, as he answered me. "Ya' can't ride on the sidewalk. Everybody shovels!"

Silly me, like that makes it okay to go sledding in the street. I replied, "Well clean up and come back down to eat. Bring Shannon down with you."

"Okay," he said. He took his boots and jacket off and almost tripped over Buster in the middle of the kitchen floor. Seeing that, I said, "Okay, Buster. You have to move" which he did, right over to his dinner spot under the table where KC sat. That's where most the food dropped. Okay, I'll be honest here. It was between KC and I. Shannon barely left a crumb where he sat.

KC went upstairs and I finished pouring the glasses of milk and set the Parmesan cheese on the table. We were having spaghetti tonight and I had my special sauce staying warm in the pot on the stove. I hollered up the stairs, "You guys coming down? Everything's ready."

And there it was—the thundering of feet coming down the steps. I really wish I hadn't ripped the carpet out. Similarly, as Buster and the boys kept me on my toes, I have to return the favor and keep them on their toes, otherwise you fall into a rut. Can't have that. Tonight it was my turn.

I purposely kept the sauce on the stove and the noodles draining in the sink so I could dish everything up for them. I grabbed a plate and put some noodles and sauce on it.

"Here ya go, Shannon," I said as I turned and handed him his plate.

Before I dished up KC's spaghetti, I set this really huge, plastic fly on his plate and buried it under the noodles. Then I spooned some sauce over it and made sure there weren't any legs sticking out from underneath.

"Here KC," I said and handed him his plate. Since I only had one bug, I kept Shannon on my list for next time. I had to keep it fair.

KC attempted to wind up some noodles around his fork. I watched him as he finally got a forkful and slurped it in his mouth, leaving a little sauce on his chin. He then took his fork and proceeded to mix the sauce into the noodles. Suddenly, he stopped and pulled the fly out from under his spaghetti by its leg. I tried not to notice as he held the thing up with noodles hooked on its wing and more that hung from the legs.

He looked at me and said, "Nice try, Mom."

Damn. That was not the reaction I had hoped for. Shannon looked at KC while he held the fly up and wrinkled his nose.

I looked at KC and said, "Ya' gotta admit, it's pretty disgusting."

They're just no fun at all. I'll have to try harder. I resumed eating my spaghetti and noticed Buster half snored under the table. I didn't mind. He always laid on my feet and kept them warm. I waited a few minutes for KC to get a few bites of food in him, then looked at him and said, "So ... tell us about your sled ride."

He finished chewing and started talking. "You wouldn't believe it. That stupid dog almost killed me. First, he went flying down the alley, well, after he sniffed a couple of garbage cans. He came out at the other end of the block and took off to the left on the boulevard. He kept going right over the big snow bank at the corner!"

We had quite a bit of snow so far that winter and the snow banks that lined the sides of the streets were at least three feet or higher. He took a couple of bites of food before he continued.

"I flew over the snow bank and barely touched the snow. I hit the ground and then he turned left again and started going down the middle of the street." (Luckily, it was a one way street and he was going the right way). He took a drink of milk and he continued.

"He was flying and going back and forth from one side of the street to the other. He bounced me off a couple of parked cars! Then he decided to jump over the snow bank in front of Josh's house" (directly across the street from our house). I was astonished there weren't any broken bones. He took another bite of spaghetti and continued his tale.

"He kept going and went around the corner and bounced me off a tree when he went up in the yard at the corner house. I flew off the sled and he just stood there and looked at me. Then we came home."

51

"That's quite the ride. Why didn't you jump off instead of flying over snowbanks and bouncing off cars?" I asked.

"That wouldn't be any fun," he replied.

Shannon shrugged and I just shook my head. What could we say?

CHAPTER 9

ANTEATER SPOOK

Life went on with the usual yelling and banging of objects as the boys and Buster chased each other through the house and up and down the stairs. Did I mention I wished I hadn't ripped the carpet out? I really have to do something about that. The boys thought it was especially funny to put one of their hockey socks on Buster's head. It made him look like an anteater. They laughed and giggled while he whipped his head around trying to throw the sock off. If that wasn't enough, they closed the door in the hallway and called him so he walked into the door.

"Not nice," I said. "Quit being so mean. He *will* pay you back someday."

Even though he was a good sport, I wondered if he kept score.

I had a little payback of my own. When the boys were supposed to be picking up their rooms, sometimes I noticed it was relatively quiet up there. I should hear them walking in and out of their closets, opening and closing drawers. To make sure they stayed on task, I opened the hall door and hollered up the stairs.

"Are you guys picking up your rooms?" Of course they always said "yes."

"Doesn't sound like it. You have thirty seconds, then I'm sending Buster up to help!"

I loved doing this because they knew anything on the floor was fair game for Buster. Toys, clothes, whatever. It didn't matter. We found that out the hard way one day when my son came running in the front door.

"Mom, something's wrong with Buster. He's having a really hard time pooping."

Great, I thought. *Now what kind of toy did he find to eat?*

"Okay, I'll go see what's wrong. Come on."

Shannon gave me a look like, "Why do I have to come along?"

We walked down the front steps to where Buster was tied. He really *was* having a hard time. His back was arched at such a weird angle that it reminded me of an exorcism or some other weird act of contortionism. Very eerie.

I walked behind him to take a peek, hoping none of the neighbors saw. I picked his tail up to have a look see. I didn't know what to expect, but it certainly wasn't to see a crew sock emerging! At least I think that's what it was. Knowing the length of a crew sock, I suspected it had a ways to go. Hmm … what to do, what to do.

"Shannon, grab that big stick over there."

I thought maybe I could somehow get the stick hooked on the sock and then pull it. Oh how disgusting this dog was. That didn't work at all. Poor Buster was still hard at work. Every so often he turned and looked at me with a pleading look in his eyes.

That dumb dog caused me more grief than the two boys. Well, almost. We had to come up with some kind of an idea. Meanwhile, poor Buster continued to strain himself.

"Hey, grab that other stick over there. Maybe I can use the two of them like chopsticks."

He grabbed the other stick as I looked around to see if we had an audience. My son wrinkled his nose and backed away.

"Why don't you hold his collar so he doesn't move around," I said.

He still had the wrinkled nose and didn't look too sure about the situation. Nevertheless, he said "Okay."

All right. I'll just cross these two sticks here and grab the sock and pull, which I did. After a few attempts, it was free. Buster looked so relieved. He just stood there and panted. I dropped the sock on the ground and made sure nothing was missing from it that may have stayed behind. All was good. I didn't ever want to do that again. At least he didn't have to go the vet and have it surgically removed. I looked at Shannon and pointed to the sock on the ground. "Whoever that sock belonged to, is not going to have a mate for it. That one will *not* be going through the wash!"

My son let go of Buster and said, "That went pretty good. Better than that racquet ball he crapped out. He was really crying that time."

"*What*? Oh never mind. I don't even want to know. Bring that goofball in the house. He's probably exhausted."

"Come on, Buster."

That was just another day and another bizarre episode in our life with Buster. I could never get the upper hand with him and I really wasn't sure if he was as calculating or vengeful as he appeared to be at times. Or if dogs even could be for that matter. All I knew for certain is he definitely had something rattling around up there in his disturbed brain. Most of the time I wasn't sure what. Then there were other times when I wondered if he deliberately tried to mess with me.

There was one peculiar instance when I came in from getting the mail. He had already been out, but I kept him in the house so I could keep a close eye on him.

I walked into the living room looking at my mail and wasn't paying much attention to anything as I passed by. But out of the corner of my eye, I saw Buster sitting in the middle of the floor looking up at the wall.

Now this wall did not have pictures or anything else that hung on it, so I stopped to see what he was looking at. His head was moving around like he was watching something crawling around. I looked at the wall, then back at Buster. His head still followed something.

I didn't see anything on the wall and since the ceilings were so high, I set the mail down and stepped up on the couch for a closer look. I saw nothing. I looked back to see if he continued to follow this crawling "thing." Thinking his purpose was to distract me for some reason, I thought he would have been on his way by now. Nope. Still there.

Every so often this "thing," or whatever, appeared to crawl on the ceiling and then back down the wall. From Buster's movements, it should have been right in front of me. I looked back at the wall again and hoped some creepy, crawly insect didn't jump on my face. I still saw nothing. Now that the hair was standing up on the back of my neck, I decided to get off the couch and back away. I thought if I went right behind Buster and got on my knees, maybe I'll see what he's seeing. Hmm, do I really *want* to see what he sees? It didn't matter. As far as I was concerned, there was nothing on that wall.

With the hair still standing up on my neck, I shivered, picked up my mail and left the room.

I wondered if that had something to do with that little topple on his head the day we first got him. I peeked around the corner to see if he moved yet. He still sat in the same spot, looking at the wall. Creepy. I could never sit on that couch after that without checking behind me.

Sometime later, I bought a new couch. It was one of those large, corner sectionals with the recliner on each end. I set the recliner section along the other wall – opposite from the wall that had the spook bug crawling on it. The straight section was opposite the dining room which had an open archway and allowed enough of a walkway between the two rooms. This was the perfect set up for my payback.

My coworker tried to scare me one day with his fake spider. He had a gross looking, furry spider attached to a tube with a squeeze ball at the end. The spider was as big as a tennis ball. Our work benches faced each other so he stretched it to my side and buried the spider and tube under some of my papers. He kept the squeeze ball on his side. When I came back from the bathroom, he squeezed the ball, the spider jumped out from under my papers and that was it. Needless to say, raising two boys and a Buster gave me nerves of steel. I didn't even flinch.

"Gonna have to try harder if you want to scare me," I told him. He looked so disappointed.

"Hey ... can I borrow that?" I asked.

"Sure, I guess," he answered.

This is gonna be great, I thought!

That night, as we watched a little TV, I sat on the end recliner with my feet up. The boys sat next to me on one side. I sat the spider down by my feet and threaded the tube up though my robe. The boys were oblivious with the TV on so I let out a blood curdling scream, "AAAAAAAHHHHHH!"

They both snapped their heads around to look.

"AAAAHHHH! GET IT OFF, GET IT OFF," I screamed and pointed to my feet.

In an instant, Shannon flew up and over the back of the couch. He touched nothing in the process until his feet hit the floor in the dining room. I looked at KC.

"AAAAHHHH! KILL IT! HIT IT WITH THIS!" I screamed and handed him the *TV Guide.* He straddled the back of the couch, rocking side to side, undecided if he should kill it or jump off the back of the couch.

That was it. I lost it. I started to laugh.

KC, still straddling the back of the couch said, "Wow, that's cool. Can I have it?"

"No. I have to take it back to work."

Shannon finally came over, almost in tears, and said, "That's not funny, Mom."

"Sorry, but did you actually think I'd be sitting here if that thing was real? No. I would be hanging from the ceiling fan."

To this day, he still reminds me how I traumatized him. Sorry.

CHAPTER 10

FARM CRITTERS

During the summer months, the boys loved to go up north to Grandpa and Grandma's house. Even though they didn't farm, they had an enormous pole barn and three acres to play in with a huge oak tree in the back corner of the yard, bordered by the neighbor's corn field. And there were even cows next door.

If that wasn't enough, two cousins lived across the road. They were all one year apart from each other. They had ducks, dogs, cats, and a horse. Their yard was smaller, but there were more things to get into ... thanks to their Uncle Brian. That was where they learned about potato guns and other types of explosive devices. I think KC came by it naturally. Thank God, Shannon had some common sense and logic, but he was also a quick learner. I'm sure, one day when they're adults, I will hear all about their adventures up north with Uncle Brian.

We headed up there on a Saturday morning and stayed 'till late Sunday afternoon. It was only an hour drive or so and since we had to drive forty minutes just to get out of the city, there really wasn't much scenery to see. Therefore, the boys had to amuse themselves. Which they did.

KC won the front seat this time. Unfortunately for me. We had just left the house and weren't even a mile down the road when he decided to start right in.

I happened to be in the left lane when we stopped for a red light. I gazed around not really comprehending what I saw, when KC said, softly said, "Mom."

I turned my head to look and he had his finger up his nose. Quite typical, actually, but he made a face at me to encourage a reaction. Of course I had to give him one. I looked back and stuck my finger up my nose and made a face back. Right as I looked over at him with my finger in my nose, KC sat back and moved his head back ... just as the people in the car next to us looked over and saw me with my finger in my nose. I could have died on the spot.

"How did you time that one?" I asked. "I'm so embarrassed. Thanks a lot!"

The light finally changed to green and I took off as fast as the speed limit would allow. That kid.

Buster knew where we were headed as soon as we reached northern suburbia. I kept the windows up enough to keep his head inside. At 65 mph, I would have had his slimers all the way back to the trunk. After KC's little set up, the trip went pretty quickly as I was deep in thought of a major payback.

Buster was in heaven. As soon as we arrived and the car door opened, he was off exploring. As we watched, the tops of the corn moved in a zigzag pattern as he disappeared into the neighbor's corn field, hot on the trail of some unsuspecting critter.

Every so often you could see him waaaay off in the distance; just a little silhouette against the sun, running this way, then that way, a 360 here, a leap in the air there. He was ecstatic.

Unfortunately, the wild critters didn't appreciate his exuberance in their back yard. Buster amused himself by annoying raccoons or pursuing little waddling, black and white critters. He must have thought, WOW, what big squirrels! From the smell of him, it was evident skunks did not like all the attention he gave them.

The boys always had a great time at the Grandparents. Grampa had an enormous pole barn filled with lots of stuff to do and things to build.

"Grampa! What's this for?" one of the boys would ask. Or, "Grampa, can we make a fort out of this?" Their imaginations ran wild. It was just as much fun helping Gramma sort through forgotten treasures lost in the back of her closet.

I heard the kids squealing and playing and saw through the window that they had all climbed up into the big tree. They were probably trying to get away from Buster. He smelled quite offensive! They wanted to build a tree house, but there wasn't enough building material around to do that. Someone needed to start a list, but my guess was no one wanted to, knowing they would then be the designated builder. It made sense. It was a huge tree and would be a major task. I managed to capture Buster long enough to douse him with tomato juice and let him go again. He went off for parts unknown. With that, I decided to see what I could do to help rustle up some dinner. Since the gorgeous day had turned into a lovely, warm evening, we decided to fire up the grill. Perfect.

As the sun started its descent, I went out on the deck and whistled for the boys and Buster.

"Coming!" the boys yelled back.

I didn't see Buster but could hear him around the corner of the house. Every few seconds he let out one of his playful barks. Wondering what kind of critter he enticed to play with him, I peeked around the corner to see five huge dairy cows. They were all lined up, side by side, with their heads hung over the wood fence. They watched as Buster leaped and jumped back and forth. The cows must have thought they were being entertained and enjoyed the show from the look of things.

Buster decided he wasn't having any luck getting them to play so, much to my horror, he ducked under the fence. This can't be good. I've heard about dairy cows not being able to give milk if they're stressed or upset. *Shoot!*

I jumped off the deck and headed toward the fence. The cows turned and ran with Buster at their heels. I envisioned a very irate farmer coming out of the house with a shotgun.

"BUSTER, NOOOO! BUSTER COME! BUSTER! COME BACK HERE!" I yelled.

He didn't even turn his head. I watched, dreadfully, and contemplated the outcome of his latest diversion. Everything seemed to move in slow motion.

What I saw next was plain ridiculous. The lead cow had stopped but the rest of them collided into each other like dominoes. I only thought this happened in cartoons ... I had to laugh. While I chuckled at the silly dairy cows, they all turned around and were now chasing Buster! I couldn't believe it. Buster ducked back under the fence. The lead cow once again stopped at the fence and the rest slammed into him again. Buster barked and danced for them as they lined up next to each other, along the fence to watch. I was astounded. This dog turned everything into a game. As if that wasn't enough, they did it again, only this time the cows turned and ran before Buster ducked under the fence. Apparently they caught on to his little game and wanted to play, too.

Buster took off after them, but this time the cows stopped and turned themselves around without slamming into each other, and chased him back to the fence. After they chased each other back and forth a half dozen times, the cows lined themselves up at the fence again. All eyes were on Buster as he stood on his side of the fence looking back with his tongue lolling out to one side. I guess they were taking a break. *Now would be a good time to grab Buster,* I thought. I managed to drag him up on the deck and gave him another dousing of tomato juice. And that's where he ate his dinner and remained out there 'till he dried off.

Sunday morning promised to be another gorgeous day. The kids headed off for their favorite tree with Buster at their heels, that is, once we hosed off the tomato juice. He looked interested for a second then headed off toward the big pole barn.

By the time we were ready to head back, the sun had started to set. I whistled for Buster again. We could see him zigzagging back through the corn, reverse of when we arrived, only a little less energetic. This should make for a serene couple of days.

We grabbed our bags and walked to the car to put them in the trunk. I looked at the boys and asked, "You got everything?"

Shannon replied, "Yeah, I think so."

"Are you leaving any and all critters and bugs here?"

"Yes," he sounded exasperated.

I specifically looked at KC.

"What about you?" I asked.

"Yeah, I have everything."

"No," I said, "Are you leaving any and all moving creatures here?"

He looked irritated, "Yes!"

"Okay. Good. Give Grampa and Gramma a hug. Buster, get in the car."

I opened the back and he was only too glad to hop in. He had put on a lot of miles in the last two days.

"I call shotgun," KC said.

"What a minute. It's Shannon's turn."

"Okay, fine," KC said.

I looked at Shannon and gave him a look.

"And don't try anything," I said as I remembered the horrific incident leaving town.

"What? I didn't do anything," he replied.

We finally backed out of the drive and waved goodbye. It was a peaceful ride home. After all the fresh, country air, we were all pretty tired by the time we arrived. Especially Buster.

CHAPTER 11

SQUIRREL LOGIC

The new life that came with spring, also brought the squirrels that scurried around in my back yard trying to remember where they buried their nuts from last fall. Buster wanted to help them. He sat for hours and watched them through the storm door. He whined … "pleeeeease let me out."

It didn't take long for the squirrels to figure out they were safe as long as Buster was on the other side of the storm door. They were so sure of it that they came right up the steps and sat on the porch, barely a foot from the door, and stared back at him through the glass. The poor dog. To save his insanity, I pulled him away and shut the door.

"Come Buster. Want a treat?" I asked. That perked his ears up. Squirrel? What squirrel? I said the "T" word. I walked over to the cupboard and grabbed him a Graham Cracker. He loved them. I even spread a little butter on it.

"Here ya' go," and gave him the cracker.

I wasn't sure if the shoestring slimers were left over from the squirrel watching or from the cracker. Either way, I pulled them off with a paper towel.

Just then, the boys stumbled in the door and headed upstairs.

"What are you guys doing?" I asked.

"Nothing. We're just gettin' some cars to play with."

"Oh, okay."

Two minutes later, they thundered back down the stairs, through the kitchen and stopped at the back door. I had opened it again since the squirrels left. Buster was back at his guard post in front of the door and stared through the glass. Shannon saw a squirrel by one of the trees in our yard.

"Buster, do you want the squirrel?" he asked.

Buster's body tensed and he drooled those shoe-strings that hung on each side of his mouth. Shannon locked the door handle and waited a second.

"Get the squirrel, Buster!"

He hit the handle and pretended he was going to let him out. Buster slammed his nose into the door!

"You guys stop tormenting that dog. One of these days he's going to go right through that door. Now just let him out," I said.

They opened the door and Buster charged through and jumped off the steps, not touching either one of them. He chased the squirrel right up the tree. The squirrel sat in the tree and chattered just to irritate him. The boys went out the door.

"Hey, where you guys going?" I asked.

"We're just going over to Dustin's house," Shannon said.

"Okay. Be careful," I replied knowing that was a moot statement for those two.

They found more objects to blow up, tie up, string up, chop, bake, and set on fire, in the twenty minutes 'till I got home from work. I never understood why my coffee grinder had little colored pieces of plastic in it.

Buster stayed in the yard under the trees. He ignored the squirrel that chattered at him and sniffed around the other tree to entice the obnoxious creature to come down. After the squirrel made its way down, Buster waited as the squirrel slowly crept up behind him. When he thought he was close enough to grab him, he turned so fast that there was a split second of lag time between his head and tail. The squirrel dashed back across the yard to the first tree and scampered up the branches. Buster was left jumping and barking uncontrollably at the bottom of the tree, trying frantically to climb up. That was just the beginning.

The squirrel then climbed up higher into the branches and jumped to the branches of the other tree. Buster followed from below. The squirrel hid up there and while Buster continued to try to climb the tree, the squirrel stole back to the first tree and crept down the back side.

Still undetected, he then sneaked up behind Buster and made that chattering sound. The cycle started all over again. Buster whipped around and chased him up the tree again. The charade went on for hours. Once the squirrel grew bored of tormenting Buster, he scrambled from the tree to the garage roof, hopped to the neighbor's tree across the alley and disappeared.

That really drove Buster nuts, because he was prevented from chasing him by a fence around the neighbor's yard. As soon as the squirrel was safe in their yard, Buster trotted back home, inhaled the yard for squirrel scents and kept it under surveillance from his perch on the porch.

There was only one instance, in all those years, where he actually caught *the squirrel*. I saw it from the kitchen window. I went to the door and said, "Buster, get the squirrel." Rather than fake him out, I opened the door before he got there. The squirrel was not far from the steps. He was crouched low to the ground, and slowly made his way toward the alley. The squirrel appeared dazed as he crept on his way.

As soon as Buster dove off the step, I noticed the squirrel had an enormous bump on his head. Maybe he fell out of a tree, which explained why he seemed dazed and didn't try to run. Buster had him in his mouth in a flash! I think he was shocked that he actually caught him, because he stood there motionless. I was out the door immediately and yelled, "Nooooooo!" and jumped on his back and grabbed hold of his midsection. I shrieked for help, knowing I couldn't hold him for long.

"You guys, heeeeelp! Get out here and help me! Hurry up!"

I heard the boys barreling down the stairs like a herd of elephants. As they burst out the door, Buster dropped the squirrel.

"KC, grab his collar," I said. "Shannon, try and get the squirrel up the tree or through the fence or somewhere out of the yard."

Shannon shooed the squirrel away while KC and I held on to Buster. It was obvious this squirrel was hurt pretty bad. He didn't want to move.

As Shannon edged him toward the fence, we managed to drag Buster back into the house. The squirrel made it through the fence and jumped into the neighbor's window well. Safe at last—for now anyway. We didn't let Buster out again 'till we were sure the squirrel was gone. I don't know if you could chalk one up for Buster or not, since the poor thing was injured.

Chapter 12

Game On

The boys each had their own room upstairs. They also had a bathroom and an extra room, mainly for my sewing endeavors (like I had time to do that). It also came in handy if we had a guest.

Even though their rooms weren't that big, they each had a huge, walk-in closet with storage cupboards on one side that fit under the slope of the roof. It was a perfect place to keep games and toys hidden from Buster. He loved their small action figures. He would usually put a couple of them in his mouth and run away. That normally started a war.

"Buster! Come back here!" one or both of them would yell.

I always knew what was going on by the thundering of paws and feet coming down the steps which warned me to get out of the way. Buster almost always ran for the dining room, positioning himself between the dining room table and the chaser. With his head lowered, he would peek under the table with the toys hanging out his mouth. He waited and peered through the chair legs for one of them to come after him, unless they both came after him. Then, they would split up and catch him in the middle and turn it into a wrestling match. Buster would try to escape under the table, dragging one or both boys with him and rearranging the chairs in the process.

"You guys! What the heck is going on?" I hollered from the kitchen.

KC replied, "Stupid Buster took two of our G.I. Joes!"

"Were they on the floor?" I asked.

"Yeah but ... ," Shannon said.

"Yeah but. What's a 'yeah but'?" I asked.

"But we were playing with them," he said.

"Buster, come," I said. "And don't grab him. Let him come out of there. I'll get your G.I. Joes."

Buster came out from under the table and dragged only one chair with him. I was surprised none of them tipped over. He looked rather happy, like he had won the match. I stepped in front of him and said, "Buster, give," and held out my hand. He didn't want to cooperate.

"Give," I said and took one of the G.I. Joes in my hand. "Give."

He finally figured out he did not win and had to give them back. I took them into the kitchen and rinsed the slobber off. Good as new.

"Here. All clean," I said and gave them back to the boys.

They grabbed them and ran back upstairs. I heard a door shut behind them. I guess they didn't want to take any chances of Buster grabbing another action figure.

Occasionally, I saw He-Man and Skeletor upstairs in the bathroom sink. I thought they tossed them in the sink on the way downstairs as a quick solution to keep them from Buster. But I didn't understand why they were always wet. That didn't make sense to play with them in a small, bathroom sink. And my sons took showers so I was pretty sure they didn't play with them in the shower. I was perplexed, so one day I asked them,

"Why is He-Man and Skeletor always in the bathroom sink? I know you don't take baths and play with them in the tub."

"No, we play with them in the toilet," said KC.

"WHAT! IN THE TOILET?"

"Yeah," Shannon said. "We're not stupid. We wait 'till right after you clean it and it's nice and clean. When we're done playing, we throw them in the sink to dry."

"Oh my gosh. Why wouldn't you just play in the sink?"

"It's more fun in the toilet," replied KC.

"Yeah," added Shannon. "Because it's bigger and we can make them dive off the edge into the water."

"I give up. Between you guys and that dumb dog, I'm going to go nuts."

Maybe that would explain why the toilet was plugged so badly I had to call a plumber. If he found an action figure, he didn't say, but I still wondered.

I didn't want to know or hear any more, so I decided to occupy my mind with something more reasonable like cleaning out the crack in the kitchen table. That had to be done every few months or so. Between spilled milk, crumbs, and some type of cookie dough, it could easily be an abode for some undesirable, biological activity.

It was a round, oak table and very heavy, so pulling it apart was no easy task. I had to involve my feet to help pull it apart, since my arms weren't long enough to get a good grip. After grunting and pulling and twisting, I finally got it apart. *Hmm*, I thought. *Wasn't too bad.* It was mostly on the end where KC sat

71

and the other end where I sat, although not quite as bad.

Once the crumbs and other unrecognizable matter were wiped out, I could push it back together and I would be done. Not so. The metal latch thingy would not line up and it didn't slide back together. With both arms stretched out along the crack, I used some leg action to compensate for my arms not being long enough again. I was then able to almost slide it back together, except that it was too heavy. I gave it another shove with my legs and pulled toward me.

Good. It worked. At least I thought it worked, until I tried to stand up. When I leaned on the table to reach the sides, the cuffs of my shirt got pinched in the crack. Oh no. I was stuck laying on the table with my shirt sleeves caught in both ends of the crack. Now what?

"Hey guys!" I hollered. "Shannon, Casey. Hello? Can one of you guys come down here please?"

I didn't hear feet on the stairs. I had a loud whistle, but I never learned how to do it without my fingers.

"Shannon, Casey!"

They must have had their bedroom doors shut.

There was nothing I could do about it. I put my head down on the table to be more comfortable. They'd come down when they got hungry.

After a few minutes passed I heard footsteps upstairs.

"You guys. I need some help here! Can you please come down?"

"What?" Shannon asked.

"Can someone come down here please," I replied.

"Okay. In a minute," he said.

"Now would be much better. I need some help. It's kind of an emergency," I said.

"Okay," Shannon replied.

I finally heard footsteps. He came downstairs and walked into the kitchen.

"What are you doing?" he asked with a puzzled look on his face.

"Well I'm not taking a nap," I said. "My cuffs are caught in the crack of the table."

"How did you do that?" he asked.

"Never mind. Get KC down here to help you pull the table apart."

"Okay," he said. "Casey. Mom wants you down here now!" he hollered .

KC came thundering down the steps. He came into the kitchen and laughed as soon as he saw my predicament.

"Yeah, yeah. One of you grab this side of the table, one of you grab the other side and pull," I said.

After a couple of tugs, I pulled my cuffs out.

"Thank you," I said.

They both laughed and KC asked, "How long were you stuck like that?"

"Long enough," I said.

The boys chuckled and headed out the door. Another five minutes of that and I would have had a stiff back. I checked to see where they were headed and noticed one of them had grabbed their football. I hoped their friends weren't coming over. That's all I needed was for them to elaborate on my predicament.

Usually when you have two boys, one has the brains and the other has the brawn. Mine were no different and Buster knew who had what and used it to his benefit. I did not know dogs could reason like that. Scary.

Evidently, the boys decided to play football in the yard. Needless to say, Buster was built like a canine linebacker. That was my fault. I could either have an extremely intelligent dog full of mischievous energy or an extremely intelligent dog that ran next to my car so the furniture was intact when I got home from work. Choosing the latter, Buster's muscle tone weighed him in at a buff, ninety-seven pounds.

Anyway, one of their friends came over, therefore, it was a team of three against a team of one. This could be interesting. I grabbed my video camera and went outside to sit on the step to watch. I thought there might be a dispute about who actually won, so I recorded it in case we needed it for review. Plus with Buster involved, it would be fun to watch again.

They gave me the ball to start the game.

"Ready guys?" I asked as I threw the ball out in the yard.

Buster somehow got it right away, but Shannon, (brainy son of the brains and brawn duo), chased Buster, jumped on his back and tried to sneak the ball from behind. Buster, being the quick witted fur-ball, stopped on a dime, threw his head down and flipped Shannon over his head and onto his back. Good play.

Buster ran around the yard daring someone else to try to get the ball. It so happened, the other two tried to pin him in between themselves. By then, Shannon was on Buster's back again, while the other two managed to get the ball. KC (the brawny son) got the ball and ran. Buster jumped up and planted both paws on his back. The ball went flying as KC crashed to the ground.

It wasn't over yet. KC tackled Buster's hind legs while Shannon and his friend, Josh, fought to get the ball out of his mouth. He got it. Shannon had the ball and ran, his eyes wide, as he saw ninety-seven pounds of payback gallop toward him. He passed the ball to Josh. He caught it and ran. Even though Shannon no longer had the ball, Buster turned and swung his butt around as he went by and knocked him over in the process. Was that on purpose?

Buster took off after Josh who passed it to KC. KC turned to run as Buster grabbed his pant leg and tangled his feet to make him fall. Buster must have previously seen him do that all by himself.

The ball was loose again and Buster was right on it. He picked up the ball and stood with all fours apart, the ball cocked sideways in his mouth like a big cigar.

They all stood there and looked at each other, out of breath – except for Buster. He victoriously waited for someone to dare and get his ball. Game over. No review necessary.

CHAPTER 13

HOUDINI-ISM

Now that Buster was more than a year old, he had moved on to much bigger and better methods of diversion. He had mastered the art of Houdini-ism. Remember the beginning of the story when I mentioned all of the phone calls? This is when it all started … Houdini-ism.

On the days I didn't run him alongside the car, I tied a rope to a small tree out front at the bottom of our hill, mostly so the squirrels out back would leave him alone. It was long enough that Buster could come up the hill to the door. That way he could enjoy a little peace and quiet while he inhaled the various scents. The grass was thicker up by the door and with the sun behind the house, it provided the front yard with total shade. During the hottest part of the day, it was pleasantly cool. The late afternoon glare of the sun could not reach the front yard.

When I brought the mail in after work, I loved to lay on an old couch I moved out to the porch. Once I had the junk mail separated from the bills, I listened to the birds chirping and watched the curtains softly blow with the breeze. That was when I took a quick fifteen minute nap. It was a cherished "me time" that didn't last nearly as long as I would have liked.

From my quiet corner on the porch, I could hear if Buster was up to anything. I had a small, thin collar on him with his tags and a thicker collar that I hooked to a rope—a sturdy rope. Confident that nothing could go wrong, I was free to take care of the many household chores that awaited me, but not before my fifteen minute nap.

One day after I came home from work and had already taken my mail nap, I was rustling something up for dinner when the phone interrupted me. I was so engrossed in what I was doing that I was rather annoyed that I had to stop to answer the phone.

"Hello?"

"Do you have a dog named Buster?"

"Yes, I do," wondering how on earth they knew that. I forgot about the small collar he always wore with his name and our phone number on it.

"He's been out in my yard playing with my kids for the last 20 minutes." *How can that be*, I thought?

"Can you hold on a second?"

I ran to the front door and looked out to see an empty collar hooked to a rope, tied to my tree. WHAT? At first, I thought someone had let him loose, but why would anyone do that? I ran back to the phone.

"What's your address? I'll come and get him." They gave me the address. Sheesh! That's four blocks away and across a moderately busy street. I couldn't believe it.

I hollered to the boys to tell them I'd be right back and hopped in the car to make it a quick trip. I found the house right away and sure enough, there was Buster playing in the yard with their kids. He was having so much fun he didn't notice I had walked up to the gate.

"Buster! What the heck? Get in the car!"

He bounced out the gate and into the back seat and assumed the position—elbow on the arm rest, head hung out the window, tongue lolling out of his mouth. All he needed was a pair of sunglasses. I swear he acted like a celebrity with his own chauffeur.

As I started the car, the kids all yelled and waved.

"Bye Buster. See ya', " they clamored.

That was the start of Buster's fan club; his blossoming into a social butterfly, or I should say, celebrity.

"Okay, Buster. Git," I said as I opened the rear car door and pointed to the house. I didn't know it at the time, but he would grow into that name.

The empty collar was getting to be a regular occurrence. I soon realized he was only tied up because it was his idea, and about once a month, it was not his idea to be tied up.

The first time, I thought was a fluke. The second time, I tightened his collar. I could barely get a finger between it and his neck. It didn't matter. The phone would still ring and someone on the other end would ask the same question.

All right. This has gone far enough, I thought to myself. *I have to put a stop to this.*

On the way home from work the next day, I stopped at a pet supply store and picked up a choke chain. Once I figured out how to get it from a single chain to a round shape, I held it up around my hands to get an idea of how big I needed it. That was easy. I knew exactly how big I needed it for many times I had my hands ready to wring his neck.

I got home and found Buster sacked out on the floor. He opened his eye and closed it right away as I stepped over him.

"How come you're not out with the boys, Buster?" I asked.

He snorted a quick snort. That could mean the boys are up to no good if the dog had to stay home. The snort must have meant he wasn't too happy about it, either.

"Look, Buster. I got you a present," I said and took the chain out of the bag.

He gave me his undivided, Buster attention—he let out a big sigh and continued to lay there like a speed bump.

"Buster, sit up. Look," I said and held his head up so I could slide the chain over his head.

He finally sat up and looked at me with his new chain collar on. I don't think he knew what this meant. I thought we should try it out.

"Come on Buster. Want to go outside?"

He got up and ambled over to the door.

"Other door, Buster."

That was one of the few things I taught him. The other door meant the front door.

I lead him out the front and hooked him up by his new collar. I stood there and watched him as he strolled down the hill to check for any new scents by his tree. He didn't seem aware of any differences. I left him out and went back in the house. I made a mental note to check on him in ten minutes to make sure he was still there. Different collar, same dilemma? I hope not.

CHAPTER 14

RIDE SHARE

Since I was the only one capable of doing laundry, I made the boys responsible for at least putting their clothes away. As I came into KC's room to put his clothes on the bed, I heard voices coming from the closet. I opened the door and both boys and their friend, Dustin, were all in the closet with a lamp and a small TV.

"Oh, hi, Mom. We're camping," KC said.

"You're camping?"

"Yeah. This is our tent!"

"I see." I guess it looked like half a tent since the closet was slanted on one side from the pitch of the roof. I noticed the air was a little stale making it hard to breathe. I'm sure the lamp and TV didn't help.

"Okay guys. It's a little stuffy in here. You can stay in here, but you have to leave this door partway open so you can get some air. I'll close your bedroom door so Buster leaves you alone."

"Okay," they replied.

I made a note to self:

"Self, check on the boys in about fifteen minutes." Those young minds sure give an old mind cause to worry. Their camping was a success with Buster downstairs. They didn't have to worry about their toys disappearing or being attacked by a Buster wild animal that stalked their tent. In a couple of hours, they must have become bored and thundered down the stairs, headed for outside.

"Where you guys going?" I asked when they all headed for the back door.

"We're just going over to Dustin's for awhile," Shannon answered.

"Did you turn off the TV and lamp?" I asked.

"Yep," he said.

"What about your toys? Did you pick them up," I asked.

"Ah, yeah, kinda," KC said.

All that meant was no, they did not, so I shut the hall door to keep Buster downstairs. Sometimes he liked to snoop around up there when the boys weren't around to see what he could confiscate.

All seemed to be going well with him lately. He hadn't taken himself for an outing since I put the choke chain on him and it had already been a couple of weeks.

With other issues that preoccupied my mind, I pretty much forgot about Buster and his AWOL-edness, at least 'till the phone rang one afternoon. I could not believe what I heard. Same question, same reaction. I ran to the door to see the choke chain clipped to the rope, tied to the tree, no dog in sight.

"THAT DOG GONE DOG!"

The only thing I thought I could do to help put a stop to this, is run him alongside the car more often to wear him out. I made myself a schedule to run him every other day. I only succeeded in training him. He became stronger, faster, and more muscular. Faster than a speeding bullet. More powerful than a locomotive. Able to leap tall buildings in a ... No. But he was a Superdog. I had created a monster. Even though I kept a close eye on him, I continued to get a phone call every few weeks. Until ... it went to the next level.

Instead of the phone ringing more with the latest Buster sightings, he began getting rides home. It became almost as frequent as the phone calls.

"Mom, the cops are here," one of the boys reported from the front porch.

Now what? I thought to myself and went to the porch.

I looked out the window and down at the street. There he was, in the back of a police car. I could tell by the way he was leaning against the door with his head out the window that he had his elbow on the arm rest. That dork. Now he's a delinquent and couldn't be happier that he got a ride home from a couple of nice guys. That just frosted my cake. He got a Ride Share from the local police department.

I passed Buster on the steps on my way down to talk to the officer.

"Good evening, ma'am," he said.

"Hello. Looks like you found my dog," I replied.

"Yes, ma'am. He was running at large a few blocks from here."

"Oh boy. I had him hooked up to this rope and choke chain right here," I explained as I held up the rope.

The choke chain slipped out of its loop and hung in a single chain, still attached to the rope.

"I don't know how he got out of this," I said.

I don't think he believed me from the look on his face.

"Well, just try to keep him contained," he said and got back in the car.

"Yes sir. I'll try. Thanks for bringing him home," I said and waved. I ran up the steps to the house and yelled, "BUSTER!"

If I were going to stop his AWOL attitude, I needed to see how he was getting out of that choke chain. I tried to catch him for months. About the same number of times I tried, the cops brought him home. That's when I started calling him "The Dumb Dog" – just because he was so irritating.

As the months passed, his little jaunts got farther and farther from home. I started keeping a record to see if there were some kind of pattern. Not only was there a definite geographical pattern, but there was a pattern to the time intervals that he would disappear. About once a month, he made a counterclockwise trek to five or six different houses. He started from two or three blocks from home and worked up to seven or eight blocks away. The phone calls were on a schedule, too. Oh yeah, he knew what he was doing.

It was similar to a lodge meeting, bowling night, or an AA meeting. Did he start his own club? Or maybe it was a DD meeting—Delinquent Dogs, but as far as I knew he was the only delinquent dog in this neighborhood. The dogs I noticed around here behaved like normal dogs. But Buster was not normal. Once again, I was reminded of that little topple on his head at the breeder's house.

Not only did Buster have the uncanny ability to escape whenever he desired and from whatever he was confined to, but he was quite the thief as well. I was continually picking up toys and asking the boys, "Where did this come from?" or "Is this yours?"

Neither one of them admitted to any of it, probably because they often resembled toddler's toys. Occasionally, when I stepped out to get the mail,

I found a weird toy in the front yard. I really started to wonder when I found a pool toy. We didn't have any pool toys because we didn't have a pool. I looked over my shoulder at dear old Buster. He sat there on the porch, looking oh, so sweet and innocent. Hmm ... I filed another psychological note and wondered how much detective work I had to do. It was only a few days later I happened to find a revealing clue.

Saturday morning had started off gorgeous, but promised to be sweltering by the afternoon. I decided to run to the grocery store before it became too hot. The boys were camped in front of the TV watching cartoons. I let them watch cartoons on Saturday, but only 'till about eleven. Then they were booted outside for some fresh air and exercise. Unless it was raining or severely cold. No prolonged couch potatoing here.

"Hey guys. I'm going to run over to the store. I'll be back in about an hour, okay?"

"Okay," Shannon said. KC was too engrossed to answer.

As an afterthought, I added, "And keep Buster in the house."

Shannon replied, "Yeah, okay."

Everything should be fine for an hour. I really despised shopping, so an hour was more than enough time for me. I went out the back to the garage and hopped in the car. I drove out of my alley and headed down the street. Coincidentally, I turned my head as I was passing the house on the corner, across the street from us. There in the back yard was a small kiddie pool with a few toys scattered around it. I wonder ... I had to keep an eye on that. I hoped the neighbors didn't think I was casing out their back yard, even though that's what I was doing.

CHAPTER 15

THE SCALLYWAG

Meanwhile, the phone calls continued to come in about once a month. It wasn't an uncommon sight Saturday morning to see me as I walked down the street with a cup of coffee in one hand and a Milk Bone in the other.

After I walked the four blocks to Buster's buddy's house (where two black labs lived), I knocked on their door. I discovered that on a few occasions, and this was one of them, Buster had arrived virtually undetected. Apparently, their labs alerted their two boys that Buster had come to visit. The boys let him in and then they all ran upstairs to their room, like they had their own private club. I think he knew more people in the neighborhood than I did. In fact, I'm sure of it.

Once I drove by a corner and spotted a little kid with his mom. The little kid pointed and shouted, "Look, Mom, there's Buster!"

The kid was so young I could hardly understand him. The mom looked as astonished as I did. All I could do was look at Buster in the back seat (elbow on the arm rest) and shake my head. He sat in the back seat like he was making the rounds to survey his doggy domain and their people. I was nothing but his driver. Okay, that's gone about far enough. I had to put a stop to it and get him under control before I get in trouble. I had to be more aggressive and consistent in my surveillance. I had to find out how he is getting out of that choke chain.

One Saturday morning I was determined to keep a close eye on him. He was hooked up in the front and I made sure I checked him every five minutes or so. About the fifth trip out to the porch to look out, I realized I was too late. The empty choke chain laid on the ground by the tree. It was only five minutes since I last checked. I looked at the rope to see which direction it was pulled from the tree. It pointed toward the corner closest to our house, so I assumed that was the direction he headed. However, I've been wrong before when I tried to figure him out.

It was a beautiful, Saturday morning. It was so quiet and peaceful. I could hear the different birds chirping their songs back and forth to each other. The squirrels chased each other around and around and up and down the trees. It was warm, but not humid. A gentle breeze occasionally blew through the windows and there wasn't a cloud in the sky. Perhaps a perfect morning for a little dip in the pool? Maybe that's where he disappeared to. I quietly slipped out the front door and walked down the steps and crossed the street.

My house was the third house from the corner, so I crossed the street first to stay out of sight, then walked to the corner house. That's where I previously saw the kiddie pool on my way to the store.

Slowly, I crept along the side of the house and listened. I moved a little closer to the corner at the back of the house and stopped again. I heard splashing noises. It was a little early and a little chilly for their little kids to be out in the pool. I peeked around the corner and wasn't too surprised at what I saw. Was that my dog? Sure enough. Buster stood in the middle of their pool. Water dripped from a toy he had in his mouth. Busted! As soon as he saw me, he bounded out of the pool and took off running.

"You better be running home!"

That little thief. I bet that's where all those strange toys in the yard came from. So now he's stealing from the neighbor kids. The same kids who knew and loved him and waved every time he went by. The same kids he walked home from school and played with in their yard. The shame of it all. I bet he goes over to the black labs' house to get them involved in his shenanigans. He seemed to be more secretive when he headed over there, especially since the people who lived there weren't even aware that he was in their house sometimes.

Now that I solved the mystery of the strange toys in my yard, I could once again focus on how he escaped. Time and time again I tried to catch him, but he must have sensed when I watched him because I could not catch him escaping out of that choke chain.

One day I decided to crawl up to the front door on my hands and knees to spy on him. Since our house was on a hill, it commanded a nice view down below. I was virtually undetected from down on the walk.

"What are you doing, Mom?" Shannon asked as he walked out on the porch.

"Shhhhhhh. Buster has one get-out-of-jail-free card left. If I can't figure out how he gets out of that choke chain, the police said they were going to give me a court summons and I'll have to go to court to explain how this dumb dog gets loose. Since I can't, I'll be the one in trouble."

"Oh. Good luck with that," he said as he made a quick exit. No good. Buster must have heard us whispering. He gaped up at the door with that happy, retarded look and grinned at me with his tongue lolling out to one side. I think I'll take him for his little run alongside the car. That should take his mind off his social business.

I got up and walked outside.

"Come on, Buster. Wanna go for a ride?"

Buster didn't move and stared at me with that goofy grin.

"Buster! Come! Let's go for a ride!"

He finally trudged up the steps so I could unhook the rope. I held on to his collar and walked him to the back to put him in the car. He hopped in the back seat as soon as I opened the door. I ran in the house for my car keys and hollered for the boys,

"You guys, I'll be back in about twenty minutes. I'm taking Buster to the park."

There wasn't an answer so I knew the boys were already outside somewhere. We drove to our special spot in the back of the park. I let him out and he headed up the hill to run from tree to tree 'till he could hardly carry himself back to the car. That was a good twenty minutes of non-stop galloping, trotting, and loping along. As Buster lumbered down the hill, I got out and opened the back door for him. He climbed in – all of him, so I didn't have to lift his back end in the car. Another twenty minutes or more and it would have been a different story.

As we headed for home, I glanced in the rear view mirror and saw that he looked relaxed. He had his elbow on the arm rest and his head inside the car as he looked out the window at the scenery. He'll be good for a few days—hopefully.

CHAPTER 16

OF CHAIN AND LEATHER

In the days that followed, Buster behaved himself and stayed close to home. That made me almost as nervous as when he was AWOL! He must have something big planned. My radar was on alert and I stepped up my undercover work as I tried to catch him taking that choke chain off.

Some days I hid behind the curtain for almost half an hour, 'till one day, I saw him doing something quite strange. I watched him as he walked backward. What the heck was he doing?

I watched him intently until the rope was taut. Then he took a couple of steps forward loosening the tension a bit on the choke chain. What was he doing? He put his head down and released more tension. Wait a minute, he's going for it! I watched in anticipation. With the choke chain now slack, I saw his front paw go up to his neck. I jumped out from behind the curtain and opened the door.

"Don't even think about it."

He looked up at me, flicked the chain off his neck, and stood there, feet apart and ready to bolt.

"Don't you dare. Buster come!"

He took a step toward the street, turned back with a look of defiance and was off.

"BUSTER, COME BACK HERE!" I yelled as I bounded down the steps after him.

The chase was on. He waited for me to get within arm's reach and took off again, always pretending not to notice me. I tried running away from him to get him to chase me. I tried walking backward pretending not to notice him. He was too smart for all that nonsense.

Well, I had three options. One, get the car and some tasty treats. Two, try to anticipate his first stop and catch him there. Or three, just wait for the first phone call. Treat or no treat, I didn't want to chase him farther away with the car. If he wanted a treat, he wouldn't have left in the first place. He probably got treats wherever he stopped anyway. And who knew where his first stop was, or if he would stop at all? So I went back to the house to wait for the phone to ring or a bark at the door.

Bad dog!

I went down to the basement to take some clothes out of the dryer and busied myself with folding them up. Most of them belonged to the boys, so as I set them on the stairs for them to put away, the phone rang.

"Hello?"I asked anxiously.

"Do you have a dog named Buster?" I heard the voice on the other end ask.

"Yes. Where are you? I'll come and get him," I said.

She gave me the address. Holy cow! He wandered almost ten blocks away. This was a new stop for him.

"I'll be there in about seven minutes. Thanks," I said and hung up the phone. As I grabbed my keys and headed out the door, I saw the boys next door in the neighbor's yard.

"Hey guys. I have to go pick Buster up."

Shannon waved and KC looked up for a split second.

"I'll be right back." Ten minutes later, I pulled into the garage with Buster. The boys still played next door in the neighbor's yard. As soon as I let Buster out of the back seat, he bounded next door and joined them.

On one visit by my parents, my dad brought a harness along. I had called him with Buster's measurements and he made a nice harness out of some old leather belts. He was concerned about the trouble Buster was causing me and wanted to help.

"I think this will do it," I said as I carefully put the harness on Buster. It fit perfect. I was happy that my problems were over. I put him outside at once and enjoyed myself without that nagging voice in the back of my mind warning me to check on Buster every few minutes.

The days went by without Buster going AWOL. Thank goodness. Our schedule continued without a hitch. We were a normal family now. Or maybe we were a family with a normal dog. Truthfully, a dysfunctional family with a delinquent dog.

It seemed like a long time before the anxiety left whenever the phone rang. It felt good to relax a little.

Every so often, I checked on Buster. He squirmed and wiggled and pulled, trying to get out of that harness. I watched him closely as he seemed determined. I soon realized it was only a matter of time.

Just a few weeks had passed before the phone rang. I checked outside and there it was—that nice leather harness that fit so snug, laid there in a twisted heap. He's back on his rounds again. How did he DO that? I was astounded. I made a concerted effort to exercise him more with the thought that he would be too exhausted to roam the neighborhood. For a couple of weeks he was, but then it was time for him to go on his rounds again. As hard as I tried to stay on top of it, he continued to get the upper hand. Was it that canine sixth sense? How else did he know when I wasn't watching and waiting to catch him going AWOL?

CHAPTER 17

SHOESTRING SLIMERS

Things kept on that cyclic routine like a cat and mouse game. I tried to keep Buster appeased by taking him with me on errands, knowing how he loved to ride in the back with his own private arm rest.

On one Saturday afternoon, I was on the way to the grocery store. KC called shot gun, Buster and Shannon were in the back. I was watching the road, when the boys started laughing. I glanced over at KC.

"What?" he asked.

Keeping my eye on the road, I stole another quick glance and noticed the people in the next car were laughing and pointing to the back seat. Wondering what Shannon was up to, I stole a quick peek in the back seat. I was not the least bit surprised to see Buster, our clown, claiming all the attention.

As the wind whistled through his muzzle making the sides flap, his eyelids were also pinned back and fluttering. Not only was it comical and had us all laughing, but it looked like he had a huge grin besides. That helped to overlook those long, shoestring slimers collecting on the side of the car.

Once back home, we got Buster and the groceries in the house, in that order. "Hey Case," I said as we set some bags down in the kitchen. "Can you stay in here and make sure Buster doesn't get into any of these bags?"

I didn't dare leave bags of food unattended with Buster lurking about.

"Yeah, okay," he replied.

Shannon and I finished bringing the other bags in.

"Thanks guys," I said. "Don't go too far. I'm going to throw this pizza in the oven."

"Mmmmm, good," Shannon said as he headed down to the basement. A few minutes later, he came running back up the stairs.

"Hey, Mom. There's a really big spider down by the bathroom. It's HUGE!"

"He won't eat much," I said. "I'll go check it out later."

"No, you should check it out now. It's really, really big."

"Okay. Give me a minute and you can show me where it is."

I stuck the pizza in the oven and finished putting groceries away.

"All right," I said. "Where's this huge spider?"

We walked down the stairs and just around the corner of the steps was the drain pipe that went into the floor. The floor dipped down around it and that's where the spider was. A perfect spider condo.

I leaned down and took a peek.

"Whoa, that IS a big one," I said. "Just leave him alone and he'll eat all those nasty water bugs down here."

Shannon looked at me and wrinkled his nose.

"Trust me," I said. "He'll keep the basement clean. Let's call him, Fonzie."

He gave me another look and headed up the stairs.

Little did I know how well this spider would be at cleaning the basement. I previously thought of putting a sign at the bottom of the basement steps: "Water Bug Crossing."

It seemed almost every time I went downstairs, there were water bugs crossing in front of the steps. Sometimes they were going to the right, sometimes to the left. They were always in a group of five or more. It was bizarre. I don't know where they were going. Most times, I couldn't find them once they crossed by.

It was only a day or two before I went down the basement stairs and noticed another smaller, but similar spider camped near Fonzie. We named him, Spike. Coincidentally, there were only a few water bugs making the crossing that day.

The next day, there were none and I never saw another. With the water bug issue taken care of, I wondered how to take care of the Buster issue. It just didn't matter what I did or how much I took Buster out, he continued to do his own thing. Actually, it was rather interesting to see where he went and the feedback I received concerning his exploits.

One afternoon I took Buster for a walk. (How thrilling that must have been for a dog that roams the entire neighborhood at his own pleasure).

I was picking up one of his doo-doo prizes when a guy shouted from across the street, "Is that your dog?"

Oh no, I thought. What kind of trouble am I in now? I lived about ten blocks away. How could he know this dog?

"Yeeees," I answered sheepishly.

"Do you know your dog sits on our front step when my wife bakes cookies and barks 'till he gets one?"

"For some reason that doesn't surprise me!" I shook my head. "The next time she bakes, will you just tell him to go home?"

"Sure, but he only has one cookie and leaves anyway."

"Okay, thanks. Sorry for the trouble."

We continued on our walk and eventually made it back home without anyone else recognizing us. How embarrassing to be the owner of a delinquent dog. At least no one knows who I am, so far. I had to find a way to get control of the situation before I ended up in court.

With two mature and exquisitely full maple trees in the back yard, there was no way I could put up a fence. The large tree roots were too close to the walk between my house and the neighbors. Cutting them down was not an option. I'd let the "Dumb Dog" go to doggy jail first. I couldn't think of any other options. I had the sinking feeling of approaching doom.

In the meantime, happy Buster continued with his social life. He even met a new buddy at the end of our block. An adorable Dalmatian named Bubbles. That turned out to be his new first stop.

It wasn't long afterward that the owners put up a six foot high privacy fence. I wondered … was that to keep Bubbles in, or Buster out? I went with the latter.

CHAPTER 18

CANINE CAPERS

Without having seen the police recently, I wondered what Buster was planning. Was this the calm before the storm? Usually his last time to go out was between 9:45 and 10 pm. It was dark by then so it didn't take me long to figure out that if I didn't see him by the door in a few minutes, it was because the canine containment apparatus was laying on the ground down by the tree. I didn't see him. *Okay for you,* I thought. Stay out there, then.

I have to say, Buster's timing fits his personality —obnoxious. I laid my head on the pillow and heard a bark at the door. It was an odd bark—almost distressed. He never sounded that anxious to come in before. I got up and walked out on the porch to let him in but he was so close to the storm door, I could hardly push it open. Well no wonder—two big dogs were right there trying to get in after him. I pushed the other dogs back so I could shut the door.

"What have you done now?" I asked.

As I turned around to have a little discussion with him, I heard a loud thud on the floor. Buster had dropped the biggest bone I had ever seen. Judging by the scrapes on his nose and shoulder, I'd say he got caught stealing.

"YOU! I should throw you right back out there you thief!" I scolded as I shook my finger at him. *I heard that dogs liked to please their masters. What happened to that?* I picked up the bone and pushed Buster in the house so I could give it back to the poor dogs he stole it from. They were still at the door and happy to get their bone back. I'll give Buster credit, he had no fear taking on two dogs of equal size. I wondered if he did this sort of thing for the fun of it.

After a few days, I forgave Buster for his thieving deeds, once again. I could tell he knew I was perturbed at him by the way he followed me around. I still kept my eye on him though. There were times, although not often, that he went on his little outing and actually came back home on his own, without even a phone call. On one of these short trips, I discovered he sometimes had a different agenda.

For instance, one day while he was tied up in the front, I checked on him and all was well. He seemed content. I went on about my business and let him be. About twenty minutes later, I stepped out on the porch to see what he was up to, if anything. My first glance went to the tree to check the status of the harness—whether a dog was attached to it or not. No Buster. As soon as I felt that impression of dread wash over me, I caught a glimpse of movement off to my left. There was Buster laying in the grass. He was totally engrossed in chewing on, what looked to me, a brown bicycle seat. What the heck did that thieving fur bag steal now?

I stepped out the door and over to where he laid and bent over him to examine his treasure to see if it was, in fact, some poor kid's bicycle seat. Nope. He had an entire butt end of a ham. About seven or eight pounds of it!

"Oh, my God, Buster! Where the heck did you get that?"

I had visions of him running across someone's table and snatching it right off their platter. *Oh no. This is bad,* I thought. I quickly scanned the area to see if someone had followed him. I had another fleeting vision of Animal Control coming up the steps with one of those long poles with the loop on the end. I have to stop thinking so much.

"Buster! Give me that ham before we both go to jail!" I said.

I reached for the ham and he growled at me.

"Whoa ... did I just hear you growl at me? Not happening, Buddy! Give me that!" I said and grabbed the scruff of his neck. I picked up the ham up and took it to the trash can out back. I noticed he was right at my heels – and very attentive. Since I knew he was watching my every move, I relocated the trash can to the garage and shut the door. Mental note: make sure I tell the boys to leave the trash can in the garage and keep the door shut at all times. Buster will be watching—and waiting.

After that little escapade, I decided to keep Buster in the house for a couple of days where I could keep tabs on him. I'm sure he felt pretty bad about losing his precious dinner and may have thought he needed a little canine company. Halloween was coming up in about two weeks so I busied myself with plans to pick up some candy and get ideas for costumes. I managed to pin the boys down during dinner one night to see what they had in mind.

"So ... what are you guys going to be for Halloween this year," I asked. Shannon shrugged and KC gave me his answer through a mouthful of mashed potatoes. It sounded like, "I don't know."

"Well don't wait 'till the last minute because I need time to pick things up if you need anything," I said.

"Oh! I know what I can be," Shannon said. "I have some stuff I can use to be Pee-Wee Herman."

"Really," I replied. "Okay. What are you going to use?"

Shannon replied, "I have an old white shirt. All I need is the red bow tie."

"We'll have to find something you can use for the jacket," I said. "It'll be dark so it won't be too critical," I said.

Just as my wheels started turning to figure out what he could wear for a jacket, KC came up with an idea.

"I got it! I wanna be Rambo!"

"Wow. You two will be quite a pair," I said.

"Yeah, that's gonna be so cool. I got all kinds of ideas of what I can do to Pee-Wee!" KC said. "I need some black stuff to put on my face. And a camo bandana."

"Okay. Now we're cookin'! Sounds like a plan." I turned to Shannon, "So, do you need anything for your costume?"

"I just need something to make a red bow tie out of," he replied.

"That's no big deal," I said. "I have lots of leftover material and I know I have some red pieces."

"Okay," Shannon said.

KC was shoveling the last of his dinner in his mouth when I told him, "I'll pick up your black face paint this week. Not sure about the camo bandana."

I might even try to find something for Buster to wear if I could be sure he wouldn't knock the trick or treaters over trying to grab their candy or get out the door—or both. It would probably be a really smart idea to keep him out of sight.

Sunset comes too quick this time of year. After a quick dinner of leftovers, I helped the boys get ready for Halloween. Shannon's bow tie looked good, but something was missing. Oh, I know. I smeared a tiny bit of lipstick on his cheek bones then wet his hair down and parted it on the side. That was it. He looked quite convincing.

"Hey Case!" I hollered up the stairs. "You ready for your face paint?"

He came down the steps like he was half falling down. (He probably was). He had jeans and a white T-shirt on. I found a black piece of material for a headband and tied it on. I randomly smudged black face paint on his face and he, too, looked quite convincing. They were ready.

"Let's get a picture of you two," I said. "Go stand over there" and pointed to the wall by the table.

As I looked through the viewfinder, I saw Rambo's arm around Pee-Wee's neck and a gun pointed to the side of his head.

"Don't you two look like a pair. A pair of what, I don't know." I snapped a few pictures. I even got one of Pee-Wee with a choke hold around Rambo's neck and the gun to his head. They were ready for Halloween.

"So you guys check in every time you go around a block. And don't eat anything 'till you get back here and check things over, okay?"

"Yep. See ya' later, Mom."

"Be careful," I said as they headed out the door.

As requested, the boys went around the block and checked in. After about an hour, they returned from their third trip, and said they wanted to stay home and hand out the candy. I wondered what that was about. Didn't seem right, but I needed a break. I went in the house and sat down in front of the TV for bit. It sounded like there were still a lot of kids coming and going. About twenty minutes later the door opened and Shannon poked his head in.

"Mom, some guy wants to talk to you."

"What? What does he want to talk to me for?" I asked.

"I don't know," Shannon replied.

I got up and went out on the porch. Sure enough a guy stood on the steps with his two little kids.

"Hi. What's going on?" I asked. He was a rather large man who didn't look familiar to me.

"I want to say what your boys are doing isn't very nice," he said.

"What do you mean? What did they do?" I asked and shot them a glance.

"They put candy in the kid's bags that was tied to a string, then yanked it back out when they walked away."

"What?" I turned to the boys and they sat there with dread in their eyes. "Is that what you guys were doing?"

They both answered barely above a whisper, "Yeah."

I looked at the boys. "Do you two have something to say to these people?"

They both replied, "Sorry."

I looked at the guy and said, "I'm so sorry about this. I had no idea. Here's their candy." I gave them two handfuls.

"Thanks," he said and left.

"Get in the house! What the heck were you thinking? Why would you do something like that?

Don't answer. That was just plain dirty, sneaky, rotten and mean!"

That was an unforgettable Halloween. I wondered if they took lessons from Buster? I should have known better than to leave those two alone, unsupervised, for more than twenty minutes.

CHAPTER 19

SCHOLASTIC SPASTIC

With another year almost gone, Buster was almost three. He was an older, wiser, Buster. He certainly had the wiser part down and that's what worried me.

Winter was fast approaching and the days were colder now. My Maple trees in back did their spectacular transformation and were almost completely bare now. The shade they provided on those hot, summer afternoons, was well worth the work when they dropped their leaves. I loved that time of year. Cooler days, even cooler nights. Buster loved it, too.

One day, Buster left on his rounds and didn't come home. When I noticed that Buster was gone and the phone hadn't rang, I got a list of all the Shelters, Animal Control, everything in the area and called on a regular basis. We put up fliers and searched the neighborhood. No one had seen him. I took detours whenever I was running errands and looked for him. Nothing.

Then one Monday after work, there was a strange message on my answering machine. A lady called and asked if I had a dog named Buster and left her number. I called her back and said that I had a dog by the name of Buster, but he ran off a couple months ago. She asked if I could describe him, which I did. I was starting to get anxious, wondering if she knew of his whereabouts.

She said, "If that's him, he's in Mankato."

"Mankato?!" That's about a hundred miles away! How on earth?

I told her where I lived and it happened that she lived about three miles away. Evidently, he just showed up one day. Because of her dog, she couldn't keep him inside, so her son took him to college. If it were Buster, he had to cross a busy street. That was something he hadn't done before. But with him, anything was possible.

She told me her son would bring him back the following weekend and we could see if it were Buster. Hmph! Now he goes to college—to what—polish his social skills? Maybe he should take an English class.

Friday finally arrived. We had the address and were on our way to see if our long, lost Houdini made it back.

On the way over, I tried to find the path he could have taken. It must have been easier for him because we kept running into dead end streets. There were just as many streets that were quite busy, too. I don't know how he does it.

We knocked on the door and held our breath. As soon as we spoke, the dog came bounding to the door. The next thing I heard was my boys yelling, "Buster!" I chatted for a few minutes with Buster's roommate from college. It sounded like he was one of the guys and had a great time. There's no doubt in my mind that he did.

I gave his college roomy some money for the food he bought and loaded Buster in the car. I glanced at the guy and he didn't seem too sad to see him go. Wonder what happened? Rather than get any more details, we left instead.

We pulled in the drive at home and let Buster out. He bounded to the door and as soon as we opened it, he found a spot to sprawl out on the floor. We were happy to have our kitchen speed bump back home again. *Were we really?* I bent down to rub his belly, this time without an ulterior motive. He seemed content and was snoring within minutes.

After a couple of days, everything was back to normal and Buster actually behaved himself. Those college guys must have worn him out. Maybe he was recovering from a bad hangover. I could see him drinking beer. Okay, I don't want to go there. I had enough problems without having to live with a drunken, delinquent dog.

The weekend came and went. Everything was going well and no AWOL Buster … yet. I knew it was only a matter of time. I had the boys keep him busy with various diversions. Actually, they were both pretty good at it. I sometimes didn't agree with their methods, but as long as no one got hurt, I could live with that.

I arrived home from work one day and didn't see either of the boys near the house. The rule was that they had to stay by the house for the twenty minutes or so 'till I got home from work, but today they were nowhere in sight. I could understand why. It was the most spectacular Indian Summer day. Maybe the last nice day 'till next spring.

As I came in the back door and went to the front porch to get the mail, I realized Buster was not laying on the floor and did not hear the boys in the house either. No one was around. That could only mean one thing – trouble. I turned to go back in the house, but something caught my eye. I stopped and looked down the street. Oh my God! I saw Buster running full speed down the street – with KC in a wagon. Shannon trailed behind on his skateboard. The wagon looked like it was going to pass Buster as it came up almost next to him. All of a sudden, he veered to the right. I saw some movement in someone's yard. Was that a squirrel? Just when I thought Buster was running full speed, he picked up his pace and went after it. KC might have made it over the curb had there not been a parked car there. Buster swerved too sharply in front of the car while KC was still next to it. He leaned precariously to one side to avoid the car.

I could hear him screaming, "Buster, Nooooo! Stop!"

You know how accidents seem to happen in slow motion? I think that only works from the perspective of the accident-ee. All I saw was that the wagon bounced off the parked car and KC flew out of the wagon.

That's going to hurt, I thought, as he landed on his palms and stomach. The wheels of the wagon broke off as it flipped over and over before it came to rest in the gutter.

I ran down our hill and across the street where he had picked himself up. Shannon rolled up with a huge grin of amazement.

"GEEZ, are you all right?" I asked.

I only saw a minor amount of blood when he answered, "Ya', I think so."

"What the heck are you doing with that little wagon? It had plastic wheels!"

He had a slight grin on his face when he said, "I know. And you can't steer it either."

Shannon laughed. I was flabbergasted and replied, "Then why the heck did you hook it up to Buster? Are you crazy?"

"No, I just wanted to go for a ride."

"What's wrong with your bicycle?" I asked.

"That's no fun to just pedal around. And Buster goes faster."

I could not believe what I heard.

"I don't know who is worse, you or Buster. Between the two of ya', you haven't got half an ounce of common sense. You're lucky you didn't get hurt any worse. Come in the house so we can pick the gravel out of your hands. You too," I said as I gave Shannon a look.

I saw Buster patiently waiting like he wanted to go for another run. The wagon laid upside down near him. I think he enjoyed torturing this kid. He seemed more than willing to run at full speed pulling KC behind him in whatever makeshift, transport device he put together.

I untied the wagon and grabbed Buster to walk him across the street and bring him in the house. He didn't seem to mind. Judging by the slimers hanging from his mouth, I figured he needed a drink. And so did I - but that wouldn't be water.

CHAPTER 20

AIN'T NO CURE FOR THE SUMMERTIME RUSE

I never would have thought that being at work all day would be a blessing, especially during the summer. Had I been a stay at home mom (like in the old days) I would have been a witness to the perilous adventures going on at home.

I didn't know it at the time, but KC evidently had a list called "Things to Let Buster Pull You With." Sounds a little disconcerting, doesn't it? I'm glad I didn't know about it or observe any of this sooner or I'd have a lot more gray hair and a lot sooner, too.

You would think Buster and the boys had pretty much "been there, done that," but nooooo. There was more. Now where do I begin with these crazy little escapades?

Ruse Number 1:
Summer was a good time for nonsense like that. You have your roller blades, cardboard boxes, wagons, bicycles …. you name it. What about something that didn't need air, a chain, oil, or a handle to steer? A metal trash can lid would fit that criteria, wouldn't it? First, one had to make sure the handle is flattened. Then all you needed is something to hook to the Buster. Beyond that, you would be good to go.

Apparently, Buster was always game for whatever KC had in mind. He stood nearby waiting for the moment when he was attached to whatever he was going to drag along behind him. The garage usually had a rope or something you used to hitch him up. Pretty straightforward and simple, right?

To help Buster get started and gain a little momentum, you could choose to head out the end of the alley that had a short hill. The only problem with that was it landed you right out into the street, without the benefit of a driver of a car seeing you because of the neighbor's retaining wall. Not to worry. There was hardly ever a car coming. Or you could head down the alley in the opposite direction. That was pretty much flat though. The last option was the big hill in the front that occasionally had a car or two, but it was a one way street so the cars only came from one direction. Either way, it was all good. Buster was up for it no matter which way they went.

As KC hooked a rope to Buster and situated himself on the trash can lid, there was one, important factoid he neglected to take into consideration – friction. Evidently, someone didn't pay attention in science class. Not having any luck getting Buster started down the alley, he did a something foolish. (Even I learned my lesson with Buster). Without any thought whatsoever, he yelled out,

"Buster, get the squirrel," and they took off at nearly full speed. That's when he learned about friction. He flew off the lid and was dragged part way down the alley before he let go. With all the protruding body parts that came into contact with the ground, he always remembered that tough lesson in physics and it was the first hoo-ha he scratched off his list of "Things to Let Buster Pull You With."

Ruse Number 2:

Another summer day, another half-baked idea in the adventurous life of KC and his demented escapades. It's back to the drawing board ... .

Taking the time to evaluate only part of the problem with the trash can lid, KC ascertained that he needed a way to get a little more momentum and dismissed the other important components of propelling himself into harms way.

About to give up on finding something to use for a Buster-propulsion vehicle, he spotted a somewhat large, cardboard box. He stood there and examined the box for a bit as his mental gears turned. Like the trash can lid, he decided he had to flatten it. Buster watched with his dopey grin. With the box sufficiently flattened and the piece of rope he used previously, KC looked at Buster.

"Come on, Buster. Let's go to the front."

Buster followed as KC dragged the box behind him. He dropped the box on the ground and sat on it. He analyzed the hill and contemplated how he could get the piece of cardboard going. One small problem – the sidewalk at the bottom of the hill.

Ah, I won't worry about it he thought. *If I get going fast enough, I'll get some air and fly right over it.*

Not only did he miss some key factors in science class – again, but he must have thought he was weightless, too. He got up and placed the cardboard at the top of the hill.

"Okay Buster. Come here," he commanded.

Buster ambled over and he positioned his body in front of the cardboard. KC hooked him to the rope and then sat on it so he could use his hands to push on each side of the cardboard.

"Buster, go!"

He gave Buster a little poke on his leg and he took off down the hill. KC pushed with his hands then grabbed the rope. He leaned back a little hoping it would help gain some speed. So far so good.

Knowing the drill, Buster kicked it into high gear. KC lurched forward unexpectedly, since he hadn't considered other components – one being the angle of the hill. Gravity and momentum had a little different effect when the ground was at a 45 degree angle. He had a hard time holding himself back to counteract the angle. Buster kept going as KC was pulled forward. He started to lose his balance. Even though he knew that Buster was unstoppable, he had to hang on to make it over the sidewalk.

Mission accomplished—almost. He tried to lift himself up as he got to the bottom of the hill to help himself over the walk. He made it halfway over but not on the piece of cardboard. That's when gravity and momentum took over. It was all knee skin that came in contact with the other half of the walk. Buster kept going and dragged him across the boulevard and into the street, but not before his elbows and chin skimmed over the curb before he let go.

Buster stopped and looked back at KC who laid half in the gutter and half on the boulevard. (I bet he had that dopey grin on his face again).

KC got up with his piece of cardboard and brushed himself off. He frowned at Buster.

"Come on Buster. Get back in the yard."

Ruse Number 3:

Since the previous incident in the small wagon with the plastic wheels, he either disregarded or forgot the outcome and decided a Radio Flyer would work better since it had real wheels, and you could actually steer it. *Seriously? Another wagon?* This time he gave it a little more thought before he hopped in and took off. Instead of letting Buster whip him around wherever he decided to go, he held the wagon handle back toward him so he could steer.

Buster watched KC as he pulled the wagon out of the garage and faced it in the alley toward the little hill. He figured that would get him some speed right off the bat.

He got the rope and sat in the wagon as he thought how to tie the handle. He needed to be able to steer while Buster pulled. After a couple attempts, he figured it out.

"Okay, Buster. Let's try it out. Come over here," he said.

Buster strolled to the wagon. He knew what to do. Once he got him hooked up and the wagon all situated with handle in hand, he was almost ready to take off. He made one last check of the rope and handle by turning it back and forth to make sure he could steer. It worked. Good to go. He got Buster going without mentioning the "S" word (squirrel). Down the alley they went. Everything started out okay, but then Buster, took off at full speed, veered left and made a wide turn and headed up the hill in the street. With that retaining wall there, KC had no idea if a car was coming or not. Didn't matter. The wagon flipped and threw him out. As they rolled into the street, the wagon was on top of him, then under him, then on top of him before he stopped.

Well that was a short trip. He made it much farther in a wagon with plastic wheels and no way to steer. Who would have thought that little wagon could perform better than a Radio Flyer? Even science didn't see that one coming.

Ruse Number 4:

The summer was an endless dream of fantastic, sunny days, and warm weather. You couldn't have ordered the days to be more perfect.

With chin in hand, supported by elbow on knee, KC sat on the back steps, deep in thought.

Okay drawing board. What next? What can I use to get some speed, without falling down, falling out or getting thrown through the air.

He reached into his pocket and pulled out the list, "Things to Let Buster Pull You With." He scanned down the items he had jotted down.

Here's a good one he said to himself. *Roller Blades!*

That was it. Continue with the wheel concept but go with a smaller device. He grabbed Buster and went in the house to get his roller blades. As long as he was there, he decided to grab a few cookies. He stood at the counter and looked out the window while he ate his favorite – Oreo Mint.

"Here ya' go, Buster" he said as he turned and gave him a cookie. The dog was a genuine garbage can. He ate anything you gave him except lettuce.

"I'll be right back," he told Buster and ran downstairs to get his roller blades.

Back upstairs he said, "Let's go," and reached for the door handle.

They went to the garage for Buster's leash this time and walked to the front. He set his roller blades down in the grass, looked around and contemplated how to get his idea from the list into the RW (real world).

I got it he said to himself.

KC grabbed his blades and headed for the steps to the front door. He retrieved his propulsion unit, (Buster) and hooked his leash to him while he sat on the steps and put his roller blades on. He thought that if he started back at the steps to the house, the house walk should give him a little more omph for take-off. *Oh boy, what did science have in store for him this time!*

With his roller blades on, he stepped down the couple of steps to the concrete walk and grabbed Buster's leash. He put his hand through the loop and held on to it then rolled to the top of the steps alongside our hill with Buster in tow. He dragged one foot sideways to slow down a little and looked down the steps to the sidewalk below.

There are times in your life when you look back at all the stupid stuff you have done and wonder, *What the hell was I thinking!?* My kids were no different and this was one of those times. They probably all were one of those times, but this one stood out from the rest.

He started down a couple of the steps and thought, *This isn't going to work*. He grabbed the hand rail and wondered, *What next? How do I catch some speed?*

He sat on the hand rail as Buster started down the stairs. He felt the paint of the hand rail as it chipped off underneath him. With only two steps left, he made it to the sidewalk as Buster gained speed. Just as he took off down the walk, Buster quickly veered to the right and jerked KC hard. He flew off his roller blades before he could react. Buster dragged him on his stomach across the street, not slowing down and KC not letting go of the leash. His hand was caught in the loop of the leash and he could not let go. Just as he got his hand out of the loop, his face hit the curb. Buster kept going.

KC laid there for a few seconds to gather his wits about him. He felt like he was tied up and dragged backward through an obstacle course. He managed to get up and felt the pain in his face. He looked around and noticed Buster a block away snooping around some bushes. He skated up the block to retrieve him and thought to himself, *This is definitely getting crossed off the list.* "Buster Come. Get back here!"

After a few more sniffs in a few more bushes, Buster strolled back and they went home.

"Dumb dog. Why am I always the one that ends up bleeding?" he asked.

Ruse Number 5:

KC occupied his time with his friends and stayed away from his list for a couple of weeks. The scrapes on his face healed and Buster was stuck at home. It was only a matter of time before KC got bored. You can only blow up your G.I. Joes so many times with firecrackers before there's nothing left.

So he found his list and scanned through it again. He chuckled as he remembered the outcome of some of the hoo-ha's he had previously crossed off the list.

So what's next? he thought. *I haven't tried my bike yet. That should work pretty good.*

KC headed to the garage for his bike. He found the leash and took it out in the alley with his bike. He wrapped it around this way and that, as he tried to figure out the best way to attach it and allow the bicycle handle to turn. Once he determined a workable configuration, he called Buster over.

"Hey, Buster. Come here."

Once again, Buster wandered over. Though he looked disinterested, he knew full well what was going to happen. KC hooked him up to the leash and secured the other end to his bike. After a couple tugs and test turns of the handlebars, he decided that this time he had a solution that he would be able to utilize over and over again ('till Buster throws him off and he has to cross it off THE LIST).

"Okay, Buster, let's go."

Buster stood there and looked over at the neighbor's yard, totally ignoring him.

"Buster, go!"

Buster didn't look like he was in the mood to run, so KC used his feet to push the bike and tap Buster in the rear. He got the hint and took off down the little hill in the alley.

"All right. That's more like it. Good Buster." KC started pedaling.

Before a few seconds had passed, he realized his configuration was only good for a straight course.

"Oh, shoot," he said as Buster took a quick left and he kept going straight. He tried leaning to get the bike to turn, but he was too close to the bushes and fell in.

Buster kept running like he was possessed. He dragged the bike along 'till he was at the next house before he stopped and turned around like he didn't know KC had fallen off. Yeah, right.

"Okay Buster, come back here!" KC hollered as he went to get him with a piece of the bush stuck in his hair. He got him back to the alley and positioned him in front of the bike again.

This time, he put the loop over the left handle grip. *Now that's a good idea*, he thought. *If I turn left, it will fall off or I can hold it on.* Perfect solution, right?

Buster took off again without any hesitation. He must have known a little bit of science himself. Instead of turning left, he made a quick right. The bike turned too sharp and jackknifed. With minor scrapes, he unhooked Buster and they went in the house. And it's back to the drawing board ... .

121

A few days flew by before KC and Buster got back to the bike-capade. He wasn't ready to cross that one off THE LIST yet.

This time, KC used a rope and held on to it with his handle grip. He could let go of the rope if he was headed for trouble. It seemed to work a little better, but still hard to control and too wobbly. He might have to give this one a little more thought. *Ah, maybe later*, he said to himself.

He shoved THE LIST into his pocket and went off to do what normal kids do on summer vacation.

Chapter 21

Bionic Buster

It was one of the few times that I had a day off. Vacation days seem to get used up quickly, but since I had a few left, I decided to take a Friday off. The weather had been perfect the last few days, I had to take a day to enjoy it.

The boys and I decided to take Buster to a large, rather secluded park that was about seven or eight blocks away. They were on their roller blades with Buster leading the way. KC had the other end of the leash and I trailed behind at a brisk walk. Good exercise for me, eh?

"Hey you guys. Keep your eyes open for you know what." I didn't want to say the "S" word. "You don't want any surprises!"

They both answered, "Yeah, we know. We're watching."

Buster hadn't taken himself on an AWOL rendezvous for a while, so he enjoyed the scents of every tree, twig, bush, and poo-pie his nose could find. His nose was like radar and to Buster's pleasure, some people didn't pick up after their dogs.

As the four of us trekked along absorbed in the gorgeous summer day, we were rudely interrupted when two large dogs ran up to bark at us. They were behind a chain link fence. Hey ... wait a minute. Those dogs looked familiar. Could they be the two dogs that chased Buster home that night when he had stolen their huge bone?

I looked at Buster as he trotted along. The dogs barked hysterically at him, but he totally ignored them as he strolled along with a definite attitude. What was that? Is Buster prancing? I could not believe my eyes.

They looked like they were trying to jump the fence to get at him. If that wasn't enough, he stopped to check out a tree on the boulevard before he passed by. The dogs went nuts.

"Hey, Buster! Friends of yours?" I had to chuckle.

He ignored me, too. Thief!

"Hurry up guys before those two jump the fence. I don't want a dog fight on my hands. I think those two are the ones Buster stole the bone from."

We picked up the pace 'till they could no longer see us and stopped barking. While we continued on, the warm breeze brushed over us like butterflies. It was such a perfect day. We were almost to the corner of a rather busy street and I could see the boys had started to slow down. I wasn't too far behind. As I quickened my pace a little to catch up, I simultaneously heard brakes squeal and KC losing his balance off the curb. Oh, thank God, he let go of the leash!

Within an instant, I heard the definite sound of metal crunching. I ran up behind the boys to see what happened. Since I am much shorter than my boys are on roller blades, I could not see what happened. The first thought that entered my mind was how the heck are we going to get this ninety-seven pound muscle machine back home if we had to go to the vet? I was horrified to think what I was about to see.

I squeezed past the boys to see a car stopped in the middle of the road. It had a dented front door and quarter panel. I thought to myself, *Oh my God! This can't be good.*

I approached the car as I scanned around it expecting to see a badly hurt dog on the ground but saw nothing. I heard barking and looked up to see Buster standing across the street in a yard. He sounded really ticked off, too. I could not believe what I saw. I ran over to him and made a quick check for injuries and even though he looked quite stressed, I found nothing. I was shocked.

The boys had crossed the street and stayed with Buster to try to calm him down a bit while I went back to talk to the nice lady who had gotten out of her car.

Buster got me in big trouble this time, I thought.

"Is that your dog?" she asked.

I guess there's no denying that one since my son was attached to the other end of the leash.

"Yes. Are you okay? I'm so sorry about your car. Looks like some damage to the front."

"I'm fine. Oh my gosh, is your dog all right?"

"He looks fine to me. Just a little irritated that his mission was aborted. He obviously had his eye on something over there," I said.

She had an incredulous look on her face as she asked, "Could I get your name and number and the name of your dog? The insurance company isn't going to believe this."

"Sure."

She handed me a piece of paper and a pen. I wrote my information down and handed it back to her.

"Just have them call me if they need to know anything. I'll be happy to explain what happened.

I'm really sorry. He must have seen a squirrel over there to make him take off like that. I'm just glad my son let go of the leash this time," I replied as I remembered KC's list.

She thanked me for my information and got back in her car. We watched her leave to make sure her car was also okay.

"Geez, Mom! Can you believe that? He's not even hurt." Shannon commented. I stood over Buster and checked more thoroughly for cuts, sore spots, and anything else to see if he reacted to any injury. I saw nothing. He appeared to have calmed down and wanted to get going.

"Unbelievable. This dog is just unbelievable! I don't get it. He should at least be a little sore and he's not even reacting when I squeeze his muscles," I said in astonishment. "Well, we're only a few blocks from the park. We might as well keep going as long as Buster seems to be doing okay. We can watch him run around a bit to make sure. It's probably better to keep him moving anyway."

The boys agreed, "Yeah, okay."

We arrived at the park a few minutes later and got Buster some water right away. The fountain squirted way out so he knew what to do. He rested for a few seconds then headed off toward some bushes. I watched him closely as he trotted along. I saw no limp or odd movements. I thought maybe he was in shock or something, but he really looked okay.

As I watched him closely, I thought *I'll check him tonight and again tomorrow for any sore spots. If he eats, drinks, and pottys, and I don't see any blood, he should be fine.*

After Buster checked all the bushes and trees and anything else that emitted a scent, we got him another drink and hooked him on his leash again and headed for home. I still saw no sign of injury.

We made it home without incident. Buster drank almost a whole bowl of water and crashed on the floor. Speed Bump. (I didn't realize how ironic that sounded). Poor dog looked exhausted. I think the trauma of colliding with a moving car took a little out of him.

Not knowing it at the time, but this traumatic incident made him a much wiser dog during his AWOL outings. He evidently remembered what happened and learned how to cross the street safely.

From then on, it was a whole new realm of canine capers. Buster progressed to an advanced level of AWOL.

CHAPTER 22

LIBERATION

Our days continued on as usual: Buster periodically went AWOL, the phone calls, the occasional ride home in the police car. Yes, I did end up going to court for the Dumb Dog, but I wasn't about to cut down my beautiful maple trees for a fence.

When the boys were older, they went to live with their dad in another state and I managed to keep Buster out of trouble on my own. We also moved not long after that. In fact, we moved not too far from where Buster was born. What a coincidence.

I worked bridge construction about thirty miles away, but was only three miles from the shop where I parked my work truck. I knew the guys there quite well since I plowed snow with them during the winter months, so I was able to let Buster hang out there while I commuted from the shop to the job site. He loved it. And the guys at the shop all loved him. He was quite a bit older now and appeared to have toned down a tad. He stayed put. In other words, you had to step over him while he napped, which was a good portion of the day. Same speed bump, different locale. Yeah, he had it tough.

But I didn't feel right about leaving Buster there every day. After all, it wasn't a doggy day care, so

I left him home on Tuesdays and Thursdays. He must have thought he was grounded. He absolutely hated it. So did the guys. I didn't gain any popularity points. He whined and barked when I left for work without him. I felt bad but he was too spoiled and had grown too fat. With a dozen guys at the shop, there was no shortage of treats and he knew how to manipulate to get them.

One Thursday, I came home from work and found his harness in a twisted heap in the drive way.

Oh, no! Here we go again, I thought.

I searched and called and whistled for him. I drove around the entire area but he was nowhere to be found. I should not have left him home when things were going so well. Like the old saying goes, "If it works, don't fix it." I messed up.

I lived and worked where the suburbs transitioned into farm country. I searched for him day after day. As it turned out, one of the guys at the shop said he thought he saw Buster in a rural area about seven or eight miles away. I was so excited that we may have found him. He said he stopped his truck, but Buster took off through a field as soon as he saw him pull over.

Sometime later the same guy saw him again, in the same area, playing in a yard with some kids. This time he got out of his truck and called his name. As soon as Buster heard his name, he jerked his head up, looked at him, and immediately took off in the opposite direction. Yep, that had to have been him. I was heartbroken. If I knew Buster at all, he knew how not to get caught. Evidently, he wanted to be free and on his own. I knew my search was over. If he wanted to come home, he would find me. As I went about my daily routine, I still kept an eye out for him, but that was the last time any of us saw Buster. I imagine he found a place with some kids to take him in. He would have made a good farm dog.

A few years later, I moved farther away from the area. I knew I would never see Buster again, but I kept the memories with me to make me smile on those days I was made aware of being dog-less.

After all that had happened - the frustration, the trouble, the blood, the stress, the silliness and the incredulity of his abilities, we still missed him and his crazy antics. No doubt about it, he definitely gave us a run for our money. I originally thought we had made him a part of our family, but it was he who made us a part of his life.

Buster, the social butterfly, playmate, thief, tormentor, delinquent, celebrity, Houdini and finally ... free spirit.

Yeah, we all missed him.

ABOUT THE AUTHOR

Kim Larson is a writer who grew up in Minnesota. Without any expertise in dog training, or without any previous experience, she found herself with the most intelligent and deliberately challenging dog ever, Buster. Not only were his adventures unbelievable at times, but they were too numerous to recount so she decided to capture them on paper. Thus, *Houdini Dog From Hell* became her first book. Through Buster's calamities and mishaps, she learned much about canine family members. Embracing the lessons she learned from his antics, she went on to become a rescue volunteer, foster mom for dogs, basic trainer, animal advocate and animal energy healer. But the most valuable and difficult lesson he taught her was *patience*.

www.ingramcontent.com/pod-product-compliance
Lightning Source LLC
Chambersburg PA
CBHW071127250626
47159CB00006B/2159